THE CANAL
MURDER

TO
DAVE & KAY

THE CANAL
MURDER

EVELYN GEISLER

Evelyn Geisler

A Division of WINEPRESS PUBLISHING

Pleasant Word (a division of WinePress Publishing, PO Box 428, Enumclaw, WA 98022) functions only as book publisher. As such, the ultimate design, content, editorial accuracy, and views expressed or implied in this work are those of the author.

Unless otherwise noted, all Scriptures are taken from the Holy Bible, New International Version, Copyright © 1973, 1978, 1984 by the International Bible Society. Used by permission of Zondervan Publishing House. The "NIV" and "New International Version" trademarks are registered in the United States Patent and Trademark Office by International Bible Society.

Scripture references marked KJV are taken from the King James Version of the Bible.

Scripture references marked NASB are taken from the New American Standard Bible, © 1960, 1963, 1968, 1971, 1972, 1973, 1975, 1977 by The Lockman Foundation. Used by permission.

ISBN 1-4141-0436-7
Library of Congress Catalog Card Number: 2005925585

CHAPTER 1

The three-quarter inch needle slid easily into my abdomen.

I removed it and patted down the adhesive dressing knowing that the very important small piece of Teflon tubing was now in place. I picked up a black card-deck-sized gizmo with another needle dangling from its attached tubing, and pushed a button. Insulin, my life juice, flowed down the tubing then dripped from the needle. I hooked this needle up at the injection site, finished priming and clipped the insulin pump to my slacks' waistband—set for another day.

The phone rang as I slipped into my jacket.

"Hello."

"Claire," my mother's voice resonated in my ear. "Have you tested your sugar this morning?"

"Yes, Mom, I've already tested. My sugar's fine."
I twisted the phone cord around my hand.

"Is the pump working all right?"

"Yes, the pump's working perfectly." Shifting my
weight from foot to foot, I rolled my eyes. "Mom,
you really don't have to call me every morning like
this. I'm a big girl now."

"All right, Claire, but you know what I always
say—once a mother, always a mother. I just want
you to have a good day."

I gritted my teeth, frustrated with her fussing,
but I tried to answer pleasantly. "You have a good
day, too. Gotta get to the office, Mom. Talk to you
later."

I sighed as I groped for the car keys in my purse.
I knew she meant well, but....

Guess it's better if she worries too much rather
than not at all. A glance at my watch told me there'd
be no time for the gym today—just a quick breakfast
at Dewey's. I locked my apartment door and headed
for the car.

A button push on the CD player and I was listening to Brahms' Fourth Symphony as I backed out
of my parking space. Sure was a good way to start
the day. I had to smile, though. Bet folks would be
surprised to find out an ex-cop enjoyed classical
music.

Dewey's was just a few blocks away. I pulled into the parking lot and headed toward the door. There was nothing special about the restaurant. It was set up like hundreds of other eateries—booths with fake leather upholstery lining the walls and tables set up in the middle—but it was my hangout, and I enjoyed eating there.

I strolled toward my usual table. A heavy-set, balding man in dark pants and white shirt, sleeves rolled up, approached me. "Hey, Dewey," I greeted him, "got anything to eat without a pound of fat in it?"

"For you, Claire, I got something really special." He grinned. "But I can't tell you what it is until after you eat it."

"Like I'm going to trust you." I laughed. "It's probably something you found in the alley last night."

"Darn, you guessed it. You ruined my surprise." Other patrons, used to our banter, started laughing with us.

I ate, chatted with Dewey and a few diners for a bit then headed toward the office.

My office is in a professional building that houses doctors and dentists. I chose the location so it would be easy for clients to walk into my office without attracting attention. After all, they could always say they were there to get a root canal rather than to check on a cheating spouse.

I walked down the hallway and paused in front of my door. The placard next to the entrance always gave me a little burst of pride—Claire Burton, Private Investigator. I sighed as I unlocked the door. How long could I keep this office open? I'd gotten a few jobs serving papers and doing background checks and insurance work since I'd quit the force, but it wasn't enough to keep me going for very long. The big agencies had most of the work sewed up. My savings were dwindling. My health insurance was about to expire, and I only had one job left to do for an attorney. I didn't want to give up on my agency, but it might come to that.

I walked through the small reception area with its few upholstered chairs, small table littered with magazines, and a half-dead potted plant. *I really should water that plant.*

When I entered my office, I saw the light blinking on the answering machine. A message! Maybe a job! I grabbed a notepad and pencil and pushed the button. A female voice crackled from the speaker.

"What? Private investigator? Sorry, I dialed the wrong number." I threw the pad and paper on the desk.

My spirits fell for a moment then I started flipping through the Rolodex. Maybe there was an attorney I could call to drum up some work.

The outer office door creaked open, and I heard voices. *Yippee!* Someone had actually come into my office!

I jumped from my desk. *Wait a minute! Calm down. Walk slowly to the door as if you haven't a care in the world.* I opened my door and saw a man and woman in their mid-fifties standing by the table. They appeared tired even this early in the morning. The man had his hand raised, ready to knock on my office door.

"I'm sorry." I smiled. "I didn't know anyone was out here. Hope you haven't been waiting long."

"No," the man said. "We just got here."

I motioned toward my office. "Please, come in."

After we were seated, I said, "I'm Claire Burton. And you are…?"

"We're the Seabolds," the man answered. "Betty and Clint."

"We saw your ad with your picture in the phone book, and I thought … I thought," Betty's voice broke. She reached in her purse for a handkerchief while Clint patted her shoulder.

I handed her a bottled water. She wiped her eyes and swallowed the liquid. "I'm sorry. It's just that this is so … so hard." She tried to choke back the tears.

"Take your time. There's no rush."

Betty took a deep breath. "Okay." She clasped Clint's hand. "We thought you might be a good person to contact about our daughter since you're a woman. We thought you might have more compassion than a man."

"Is she in some kind of trouble?"

Betty shook her head no and buried her face in her handkerchief. Clint put his arm around her and monotoned, "She was in trouble. Now she's dead."

Abruptly lifting her head, Betty glared at Clint. "She was trying to turn her life around, Clint. You know that."

Clint raised his hands in front of his body as if to defend himself from Betty's words. "You're right. She was. It's just that she was a handful for a while."

"How did she die?" I asked softly.

Betty was once again able to talk. "Do you remember when they found a girl's body in the canal?"

Something clicked in my memory. "Oh, yes. I do remember that. I thought that girl's name was Cynthia Kagel."

"It was. Clint's my second husband. My first husband, Bart Kagel, died."

"I'm sorry. That must have been hard on you both. Is that when your daughter got in trouble? After Mr. Kagel died?"

"No, Cindy and I got along okay after Bart passed, but she went crazy after I married Clint. She left school and ran away. I didn't know where she was for a while."

"But you said she was getting her act together."

Betty nodded. "That's the sad part. After a couple of years, she showed up and wanted to start over. We became mother and daughter again, then this awful thing happened." She dabbed her eyes.

"I remember the police investigation. There was a big to-do over the case since the body was discovered in the restored canal. The city fathers were pretty upset."

"Yes, they investigated, but hit a dead-end. They haven't turned up anything for quite a while. That's why we came to you. Can you help us?"

I paused for a moment before answering. "I'll be happy to spend a day on this case for you. It's only fair to tell you that I won't continue to investigate if I feel the police followed all the leads possible. It wouldn't be right to take any more of your money if I find I can't do anything else for you."

After we settled the financial details, I asked, "By the way, who was handling the case for you at the police department?"

"Just a minute," Betty said as she reached for her purse. "I still have his card."

My eyes widened as I looked at the card. The name printed in black ink made me catch my breath—Donald Snyder, Detective.

"Do you know him?" asked Clint.

"Uh, yes." I cleared my throat. "Yes, I'm acquainted with Mr. Snyder."

As I shook hands with the Seabolds and showed them to the door, my heart thunked. I'd have to see Don again. It didn't seem fair. I was probably only going to get one day's pay out of this case, and I'd have to see my ex-fiancé to boot.

CHAPTER 2

I wanted to go over to the station immediately, see Don, and get it over with but decided to start on my other job first. One of the attorneys in town—a one-man firm—had a small business client who felt one of his employees was faking an injury. It was my job to find out whether the injury was real or whether the employee was trying for an illicit paid vacation.

After picking up a book of business listings at the Chamber of Commerce, I drove over to the employee's house. He was watering his lawn, one arm in a sling.

I parked at the curb and got out of my car. "Good morning. Mr. Talbott?" I gave him a friendly grin. He turned to look at me and some of the hose water came in my direction. "I'm sorry," he said and went to turn off the hose.

"Let me help you." I turned off the spigot. "Must be a nuisance wearing that sling."

"It is," he agreed. "Work injury. I'm doing the best I can."

I held out the book toward his bad arm. "I just stopped by to drop off this list of businesses, courtesy of the Chamber."

He started to reach for it, then looked at me, winced and gave out with an ouch. *Lousy acting job, Mr. Talbott.*

"Hope you didn't hurt yourself."

"It'll be okay. Just have to be patient." He rubbed his shoulder.

"How long are you going to be off work?"

"Doc isn't sure. Could be for quite a while."

"Do you need any help doing anything around here?" I gestured to include the house and yard. "I have a little free time."

"Gee, that's nice of you. There's nothing I can think of right now, though."

"Must be tough driving."

He nodded.

"You probably miss getting out, going to work, all that stuff."

He chuckled. "I don't miss work at all. My boss is a jerk. Nothing I do is ever good enough for him. I do miss bowling, though. I love doing that."

I started to leave. "Maybe in time."

Talbott walked with me. "Yeah, maybe. There's a big bowling tournament in Hartville next week. I sure would like to be in it."

"Do you think your shoulder will be well enough by then?"

"Who knows? Maybe I'll have a miraculous healing." He winked.

I got in the car and, after driving for about a block, I allowed myself to laugh. The guy actually winked. Shouldn't be too hard to find out exactly when the tournament was being held and wander over to see who was bowling. I stopped laughing when I thought about seeing Don. I'd make him my next stop and get it over with.

It felt weird to drive up to the station without a badge on, even weirder to park in one of the visitors' spaces. Several cops greeted me when I entered the two-story brick building. I waved and stopped at the desk

"Claire! How you doing?" asked the desk sergeant.

"I'm fine. Is Don around?"

"Sure. Go on up. I think you know the way." The sergeant smiled and went back to his duties.

I headed toward the stairs. It hurt a little to walk the halls. Ghosts of past cases flew through my mind. I remembered wild chases, tough busts, and the looks on the faces of the victims' families when they thanked me. Maybe I wasn't quite over leaving the force.

My mind snapped back to the present when I saw Don hunkered down over some paperwork at his desk, running a hand through his dark hair. I sucked in a ragged breath when I saw those broad shoulders again.

"Don?"

He raised his head. There were circles under his brown eyes and a day's growth of dark stubble on his face.

"Claire!"

"Looks like you pulled an all-nighter."

He motioned toward a chair. "Yeah, I sure did, and I've got the paperwork to prove it. What brings you by?"

"I'm working a case. I understand from the people involved that you were the lead investigator on it."

"Yeah? Who was the vic?"

"Cynthia Kagel."

"Oh, that one." Don blew out a breath. "What a mess. I had everybody leaning on me from the mayor on down. Believe me, I went over all the evidence with a fine-tooth comb. Talked with everybody involved about fifteen times. Everything came to a dead end."

"I know you're thorough, Don. It's just that the parents want me to make sure all the angles were covered."

"Sure, I understand. I'm surprised the stepfather's interested in pursuing the case, though. He wasn't much help one way or the other while we were investigating."

"Really? Could he be a suspect?"

"Don't think so. He and the mom were involved in planning and attending a big family reunion over in Parkersburg about the time of the murder. Took them three or four days to set the thing up, then they were with relatives for another few days. The mom swore they were together the whole time. I think he was just mad because apparently he and Cindy didn't get along." Don stood up and started toward the storage area. "I don't mind letting you know who the players were since it's a cold case. The parents would probably give you the same list I have." He brought back a box. We started digging through it and discussed the case for a while as I made notes.

Then Don asked, "How are you doing, Claire? I heard you were having a tough time." His dark eyes tried to penetrate my thoughts.

"Who told you that?" My voice went up a notch. "One of my good friends who I haven't seen since I left the force?"

"Take it easy, Claire. I'm just worried about you. You know you could have stayed on here and had a much easier time of it."

"Yeah, right." I glared at him. "They offered me a wonderful desk job after I found out I had to use insulin because I have Type 1 diabetes. They were scared to put me back on the street." I sneered. "That would have been just ducky. Me shuffling paperwork, people smiling when they brought it to me then talking behind my back." I raised my hand to the side of my mouth. "Poor Claire. Isn't it too bad? She can't go out in the field any more." I jabbed my forefinger at him. "That isn't the life I want!"

"Claire, please. The chief was concerned about your health."

"The chief was afraid to give me a chance."

He shook his head. "You're still the same. I just want to make sure you're okay, and you go off on me."

"Ah, yes." My body tensed. "You're so considerate. I seem to remember you broke our engagement in the middle of everything else I was going through."

He gestured, palms down. "Lower your voice. Everyone's looking. Besides you know we had other issues."

"What other issues?"

"You were living your job twenty-four/seven. You had to make the most busts, solve the most cases, be Miss Super Detective."

"What's wrong with that? I was in a man's world, and I had to prove myself."

"I felt like you didn't have room in your life for me."

His remark stopped me cold. I never knew he felt that way. Besides, I'd always found time for him. He was just plain wrong. "That's not true!" Heads turned as my voice went up again. "I needed you more than ever when I found out I had diabetes."

"If you remember, I went to classes with you." Don spoke quietly, patiently. That irritated me more than if he'd shouted at me. "I wanted to find out what we needed to do to make sure you were okay. But then they offered you the desk job. You got mad at the world—over the diabetes, over the job change, everything."

"Do you blame me?" I hurled the words at him.

"Not necessarily, but you've got to understand. It was like trying to be close to a volcano. After a while, I couldn't do it any more." Don's eyes grew duller, more tired.

"Now if you want to think I was a jerk, go right ahead, but that's the way I felt at the end."

I stood and leaned over the desk, looking straight into his eyes. "I'm so glad to find out everything was my fault. But you know what? That's okay. I'll just continue being Miss Super Detective. I have my own agency, so I think I'll go ahead and solve this murder. I think I'll run out and do that little thing right now."

I heard Don calling out to me as I walked, chin up, back ramrod straight toward the door. Anger burned like fire in my chest, but my eyes filled with tears. For some dumb reason I still wanted to brush that dark stubble on his cheeks with my fingertips and feel the sandpapery glory that was his face.

I decided I was too mad to drive so went to the park for a walk. *What an idiot I am! Don's a painstaking investigator.* He was probably right when he'd said everything had led to a dead end. I kicked a rock on the sidewalk. *Stupid, stupid, stupid! You let your emotions get in the way. How are you going to get out of this jam?*

Walking down the pathways cleared my head. I thought of Betty Seabold's trusting look when she first came into the office. I remembered how she cried into her handkerchief. The right thing to do—the only thing I could do—was to meet with the Seabolds again and tell them there were no leads I could pursue. They'd already lost a daughter. They didn't need to spend money needlessly on top of that.

I called the Seabolds from the cell phone in my car and arranged to meet with them at Dewey's. As I drove toward the restaurant, I realized I now had two problems to deal with. First and foremost, of course, was keeping the office open. Second, how could I ever face Don again when he found out I hadn't even taken the case? I checked my sugar before I got out of the car. It was up because of the anger and stress. This day just kept getting better and better. I'd have to give myself a little extra insulin at lunch. At least I knew the pump could handle that.

The Seabolds were already seated at a table when I entered Dewey's. While we ate lunch, I told them I didn't think I could uncover anything new about the case.

"I appreciate your honesty," said Betty. She reached into a folder she'd brought. "There is one question I have, though. Did Detective Snyder ever figure out what this meant?" She handed me a paper with initials, dollar amounts, arrows, and question marks written on it.

"I don't recall seeing this in the file," I replied. "Whose handwriting is it?"

"It's Cindy's," answered Clint. "We went to her apartment when she didn't come to our family reunion. We looked through her rooms, and this paper was the only thing we found that didn't make sense, so I took a copy of it. Then we called the police and reported Cindy as a missing person. They have the original."

"Let me make a quick call." I slid out of the booth, headed toward my car for privacy, and called Don on the cellular.

I paused for a second when I heard his deep voice in my ear, then spoke. "Don, it's Claire. Can I ask you a question even though I did act like Mount Vesuvius in your office?"

He chuckled. "Sure. I've cleaned up the lava. What do you need?"

"On the Kagel case—did you ever get a paper from missing persons that had some strange scribbling on it?"

"Let me see…" I heard Don rustling some papers. "Ah, yes. I remember that now. Never found any significance to it. I figured she wrote notes to herself about her bank account. She had an account at First Bank of Indalia."

"Thanks, Don. I'll let you get back to work now."

"Claire?"

"Yes?"

"Any chance of seeing you sometime—maybe lighting another fire besides Vesuvius?"

I closed my eyes savoring his velvet voice. No. I shook off wanting to see him. Too many things had happened between us. "Maybe later. I'm pretty busy with this case right now." I clicked off the phone.

After returning to the table, I asked, "How careful was Cindy about her bank account?"

Betty laughed. "She was very careful. I used to call her the 'little accountant'. It was a strange part of her personality, her being so young, yet so attentive to her money."

I pushed the paper toward Betty. "Do you think she would have made notes about her account on a paper like this?"

"No way." Betty shook her head. "She always entered everything in her ledger."

"Then I'll take the case. I may be able to help you. Can I keep this paper?"

The Seabolds agreed. We went back to the office to sign a contract. I told them I'd contact them soon for an in-depth interview about Cindy. As the Seabolds left, Betty said,

"Be sure you talk to that idiot boyfriend of Cindy's. He's the biggest jerk I ever met."

I assured them I'd talk to him, then went back to my desk. Leaning back in the chair, my feet propped up, I savored the moment. I had a new case, a clue and a suspect. I just might make it after all.

CHAPTER 3

I began analyzing the notes I'd taken at the station. Cindy suffered a blow to the head before she was dumped in the canal. She died by drowning, though, indicating she'd still been alive when she hit the water. The body had floated to the surface after a week or so; consequently, time of death couldn't be determined accurately.

The canal was the crime scene. I needed to check it out. I pulled my gold Saturn onto the street and headed east. The canal had been the dream child of the mayor and city council. They'd decided that if they cleaned up an old waterway that ran through the city, landscaped it and made it attractive for businesses to locate on its banks, they might be able to re-energize the downtown area. The plan had worked until Cindy Kagel's body floated to the canal's surface one morning.

I always enjoyed walking along the canal during the daytime. The wide, paved walkways on both banks made strolling easy. I examined the terrain carefully, conscious that it might contain clues. Grassy slopes with trees and flowers led down to the walkways. Bridges spanned the canal in various places so people and cars could easily get from one side to the other. Office buildings, businesses, and apartment buildings all co-existed in a pleasant blend of brick, concrete block, and glass structures.

I paused to study the water. It was a murky four to five feet deep. Cindy's submerged body could easily have gone undetected. The canal water flowed from a boat landing at one end to a park at the other, but the current wasn't strong enough to move a corpse.

I had to give the doer an A plus for disposing of Cindy's body. It would have been easy to come out at night and dump her from a bridge or roll her down one of those green hills. He might even have lived in one of the near-by apartments at the time. The convenience would have been beautiful—only a few steps from his home to the canal. There were lots of possibilities. I had to narrow them down.

I decided to go back to the office and study the list of people Don interviewed. Maybe I could pick up a clue somewhere as to what that piece of paper meant.

Of course, Don had talked to the Seabolds several times. He'd also questioned Cindy's boyfriend, Bobby Spears. A man named Harold Carpenter was on the list, too. He headed up a food bank. Seems Cindy was trying to turn her life around as Betty had said. She'd been working at the food bank up until her death. The boy friend looked like a good place to start. Before I approached him, I decided to do some checking on him to see what kind of life he was leading.

As I started making notes, I glanced at my watch. Oh, boy. Time to go to' the folks' for our weekly dinner.

When I'd moved into my own place several years ago, I'd promised my folks we'd get together for dinner at least once a week. Now it was a command performance every Tuesday at seven o' clock sharp. Since I was feeling happy about my case, I flipped a Stan Kenton jazz CD in the car's player and headed out.

My old neighborhood is a quiet two blocks long—a short stretch of peaceful street in the midst of a busy suburban area. Nothing ever seems to move there. Even the leaves hesitate to stir in the breeze. I'm fond of the timeless feel of the area.

I pulled up to my folks' ranch style home. The yard, as usual, was in impeccable order. I always suspected that my dad went out daily to measure the length of each blade of grass. No unruly tufts of green were ever permitted in the Burton lawn.

Dad was standing in the doorway as I exited the car. His name, Harvey, suited him. He was tall and quiet like James Stewart's imaginary rabbit friend, but I never doubted that my father loved me.

"Hi, Dad. How's it going?"

He kissed me on the cheek. "Good, now that tax season's over."

"Ah, yes. The accountant's blessing and curse. At least you probably raked in some bucks."

"What good's that going to do me if I have to pay taxes on it?"

We both laughed. "Where's Mom?" I asked.

"Where do you think? In the kitchen, of course."

My mom was in full battle gear, apron and oven mitt on when I came in the kitchen. She handled spatulas and knives with military precision as she put the finishing touches on dinner.

"Claire! I thought I heard you come in. Look and see what I've made for dinner. Don't think you'll find too many carbs here tonight." She waved an arm at the serving plates she was loading. Broiled fish, tomato and spinach salad with low-fat dressing, cooked fresh green beans, and mixed strawberries and blueberries for dessert. Mom beamed with satisfaction at her culinary conquest. She'd beaten back the carbs again.

"You're right, Mom. Don't need too much insulin for this meal. I'll save money tonight."

We all went to the table and began passing plates. "Guess what?" I said. "I have a new case."

"Really." Mom grinned. "Tell us about it."

I gave them the bare bones of the case. Of course, they remembered reading about Cindy in the paper.

"Wasn't that Don's case?" asked Dad.

"Yes, it was. I met with him today."

Mom was instantly attentive at the mention of Don's name. "How did it go?"

"Okay. We kept it professional for the most part."

"What do you mean 'for the most part'?" Her eyes narrowed.

"He asked me how I was doing. I told him I was fine."

She threw her napkin on the table. "Well, he certainly isn't fine. He's a creep, if you ask me."

"Ariel." Dad's fork clattered on his dish. "We've been through all this before. Claire's better off without him, if he couldn't be patient about what she was going through."

"I know, I know. It's just that he missed such a good bet." She turned to me and took my hand. "Never doubt that you've got everything going for you, honey. You're bright. You've got a great build, gorgeous red hair and beautiful green eyes. Believe me, someone's going to sit up and take notice someday."

"Thanks, Mom, but I don't need the pep talk tonight. I'm not interested in getting involved right now. I've got enough on my plate with this case."

"Speaking of plate," Dad said, "let's finish eating before everything gets cold."

I said a mental thank you to Dad and finished eating. Mom and I went to the kitchen to clean up after dinner. She began loading dishes in the dishwasher. "When's your next doctor's appointment?"

"Sometime next month."

"Will you be doing that blood test—what is it?"

"The A1C?"

"Is that the one that tells how your blood sugar control's been over the last few months?"

"Yes."

"Will you be getting that test done before you go in?"

"Yes, I will."

"Are you still going to the gym regularly?"

Okay, that's it. I closed my eyes for a second, took a deep breath, and let it out. "Mom," I motioned to a chair, "we have to talk about these interrogations I get every time I come over here."

She sat down, a puzzled look on her face. "What are you talking about?"

"You ask me questions all the time about my diabetes. You make me feel like a little kid. Sometimes I don't want to come over because I know I'm going to get grilled."

"What do you mean, 'grilled'?"

"Is the pump working okay? Are you monitoring when you should? What are you eating? Are you getting enough exercise?" I let out a breath. "Mom, it's enough. Believe me, I'm taking care of myself. I have everything under control. You've got to get off my back about the diabetes!"

Mom's eyes filled with tears. "You don't need to shout."

"I wasn't."

"Yes, you were." She reached for a handkerchief in her apron pocket and dabbed at her nose. "Do you know what it's like to get a call from the emergency room and find out your daughter's collapsed and has diabetes? I was terrified that night, and I'm still scared. I know the risks now, and I don't want anything to happen to you."

I looked at my mother's stricken face for a long moment, then hugged her. "I'm sorry. I never thought about how it affects you and Dad." She sniffled into my shoulder. "Let's try this," I patted her shoulder. "I promise I'll tell you when I'm having problems, okay? Otherwise, I want you to treat me like an adult who can take care of herself."

She nodded and washed her face at the sink. I said goodnight and went to the car. What an evening. Talking about Don and having a fight with a concerned parent. Doesn't get much better than that. Maybe my brother was right to leave town.

I went back to the Brahms CD as I pulled away from the curb. At least I had the Kagel case going for me.

CHAPTER 4

Next morning, I headed over to the Indalia Daily News and spent the morning there going over old issues of the newspaper. Of course, the paper had lots of articles about Cindy's death and the ensuing investigation. I made copies of the stories, but I was aware they might contain inaccuracies. Also, I was certain Don hadn't released all the facts of the case to the reporters. No one connected with the case appeared in any other news items.

I logged onto my information agency's Web site and typed in requests for data I needed. I wanted to know if any of the people on my suspect list had any past difficulties with the law. Other details of their personal lives might come in handy, too.

Next I called the Seabolds to set up an appointment with them to discuss Cindy. It wouldn't be pleasant. Betty Seabold was still understandably emotional about her daughter's death. However, I needed to know what made Cindy tick—what her life had been like.

I decided to tuck my pump in my bra and, instead, wear a tape recorder on my waistband for the interview. The recorder was about the same size as my pump and would go unnoticed by the Seabolds. Some people clam up when they know they're being taped. I didn't want that problem to occur with Betty and Clint. I also wanted to capture the nuances of their voices as they answered my questions.

The Seabolds lived in a bungalow in a lower middle class section of the city. A concrete curb bordered the small front lawn, and some flower-beds were scattered around the house. The few blooms present struggled for space between the encroaching weeds.

Betty answered when I rang the bell. Stringy brown hair streaked with gray framed her haggard face. She looked like she'd probably lost weight since Cindy's death because her body hung loose inside her housedress.

"Miss Burton, come in." She gestured toward the front room. It was a clutter of dirty dishes, newspapers, and mail. "Sorry. I haven't had time to clean up."

"No problem," I replied. "Please, call me Claire."

Clint sat in an easy chair, watching television. He pushed a button on the remote control to turn the set off when I came into the room. He was a hard man to read. His face was as expressionless as the last time I'd seen him. Just those cold gray eyes looking at me. He heaved his stocky body out of the chair and offered his hand.

We shook hands. I took a seat on the couch and pulled a notepad and pen from my purse. I knew the notepad would be a further diversion from the tape recorder. "Mind if I take notes while we talk?" They assured me note taking was okay.

"Can I show you a picture of Cindy before we start?" Betty asked.

"That would be great. I was going to ask to see a picture of her."

Betty went to the bookcase and picked up a silver-framed eight by ten photograph. She handed it to me. A girl in a cheerleading outfit smiled at me from the picture. She was slim with blonde hair and hazel eyes. Perky would have been a good adjective to describe her.

What a waste. Cindy had gone from being a popular girl at her high school to a pale corpse floating in a canal. I was determined to find her killer.

"She's beautiful," I said.

"Yes, she was." Betty choked out the words. Clint reached for a tissue from the box on the coffee table.

His response was so automatic, I realized he must have handed Betty lots of tissues over the past months.

I waited for her to compose herself, then continued the interview. "What was your life like with Cindy before you married Clint?"

"It was tough after Bart passed away. He died in an accident at work, so I did get some money to tide us over. Cindy and I hung in there together." Betty smiled, evidently remembering the old days with her daughter. "Eventually, though, I had to get some training in order to get a decent job. I went back to school and became a medical office assistant. Cindy was upset at first that I was working and couldn't spend as much time with her, but she came to understand that I had to pull in some income."

"Did she become a wild kid then?"

"No, she acted up a little bit, but she was in junior high school then, too. You know how kids that age are."

I smiled. "Can't say that I do personally, but I've heard stories from my friends."

"She settled down after a few months and seemed fine. Here's all the records I could find about Cindy. You can see for yourself what activities she was in and what a good student she was."

Betty pushed a basketful of papers and albums toward me. The albums contained pictures of Cindy from babyhood on. There were photos of her in grade school, at birthday parties, Brownie troop activities, in junior high, and part of high school. Her grades, for the most part, gave her a solid B average. I could see a dip in junior high, then her grades improved. High school was a different story. She started off well, but suddenly in her junior year, her grades plummeted. There was no record of a senior year.

"What happened here?" I pointed to Cindy's falling grades.

Betty sighed. "That's the year everything came apart. I need to backtrack a little bit so you can understand what happened. Please, let me get us some coffee first, though. I've forgotten my manners." She went to the kitchen.

Clint and I sat in silence for a moment then he spoke. "I hope you can put an end to this thing. I'm afraid Betty's going to have a heart attack or a stroke over it."

"I can certainly understand. Losing a child has to be the worst thing that can happen to a parent. And then not knowing who did it." I shook my head. "It's gotta be rough."

"That's true, all right, but let me tell you, that Cindy was a handful. She…." He stopped speaking as Betty entered the room. She shifted some books and set a tray with a coffeepot and the rest of the fixings on the coffee table. We each poured a cup then Betty began speaking again.

"Let's see. Where was I? Oh, yes. After Cindy got used to me working, everything went fine for a few years. I even found a new romance." She smiled at Clint.

"How did you two meet?"

"One day he came into the doctor's office where I worked. We hit it off and began dating. One thing led to another, and we got married." She took Clint's hand.

"Is that when Cindy started acting up?"

"No, that's the strange thing. You'd think she would have, since she had to share me with Clint, but she didn't right away. She was happy that I'd found someone. Besides she had her own beau. That Bobby Spears." Betty sneered. "She understood what I was feeling. It wasn't until about six months after Clint and I married that Cindy seemed to unravel. I never figured out why."

I looked up from my notes. "She didn't confide in you at all? You seemed to be a very close mother and daughter."

"That's another strange thing. She always talked to me about her problems, but I couldn't get a word out of her at that point. She shut me out."

"No mention of boyfriend or school problems? Any problems with one of her friends?"

"No, she just wouldn't talk to me anymore. She started staying away from home a lot. She went wild for a while. She stayed with Bobby some of the time.

He finally got fed up with her. That's when she lived on the street for a few months." She shivered. "I think she got the message then."

"What do you mean?"

"She found out how dangerous it could be and decided she'd better clean up her act. She showed up at the house one day after Clint went to work. She said she wanted to be close to me again."

"Did she move back in then?"

"No," Betty shook her head. "She wanted to live on her own. She was looking for a job and was planning on sharing an apartment with some old girl friends."

I continued making notes. "I'll need their names."

"Of course. Anyway, we started seeing each other several times a week."

"Did you go out as a family?" I gestured to include Clint with Betty.

"Not too often. We had an occasional dinner out together, but Cindy said she wanted time alone with me. She didn't want to share me with anyone else when we were together."

I raised an eyebrow. "That's quite a change from when you first married Clint, isn't it?"

"Yes, but I figured she was trying to catch up on mother-daughter time."

"What happened then?"

"We continued to see each other. Then about the time of our family reunion…" Betty's voice began to shake. Clint's reflexes kicked in, and he handed her another tissue. I turned to him.

"What were you doing at that time?"

Clint shifted in his chair. "It was Betty's family's reunion. We decided to have a big blowout. We were going to meet in Parkersburg and do some things over there, then come over here for an afternoon of boating on the canal."

"Sounds like a big affair. What did you have to do to prepare?"

"We spent a few days in Parkersburg making sure the hotel rooms were adequate, and the restaurants were all set up. After that we waited for all the folks to come in and helped them get settled."

"How many people did you have to accommodate?"

Clint thought for a moment. "About seventy-five, I think."

"And you were together the whole time?"

"Uh, yes, of course. It took the two of us to pull all this together."

Betty stared at Clint for a quick second, then teared up. "Claire was so looking forward to…." She buried her face in the tissue again.

Clint's face softened for the first time. "What she's trying to say is Claire was looking forward to seeing her relatives again. She wanted to be part of the reunion."

"So she was helping you with the activities?"

Betty was under control again. "No, she had to work, but she was looking forward to taking part in everything. That's why we knew something was wrong when we didn't hear from her right before the reunion."

Clint nodded in agreement. "We decided to go to her apartment to see if anything was wrong."

"Anything else you think is important for me to know?"

Betty furrowed her brow. "I—I can't think of anything. I do have a question. Did you figure anything out about that paper we gave you?"

"Not yet, but I have something to check on in connection with some of the initials. By the way, do you have another picture of Cindy I could have?

"Sure. Just a minute." Betty rummaged around in a desk drawer, then handed me a wallet-sized cheerleader picture.

I got up. "You have my card. If you think of anything else you feel is important, don't hesitate to call me."

Betty saw me to the door. "Thanks so much for your help. I feel you care."

I gave her a quick hug. "I haven't done anything yet, but I'll get started right away. I'll need that list of friends Claire was staying with. Also, could you give me the names of some of the people who were at the reunion?"

"Yes, but I don't see how they could help you."

"Just covering all the bases. I'd appreciate it if you could drop the names by my office tomorrow."

Questions swirled through my mind as I drove home. Would Cindy's friends know anything important? Would the boyfriend be able to help in any way? Why did Betty look at Clint when he said they'd been together at the reunion the whole time? And would Don be able to help me with some of the initials on that piece of paper?

I sighed. Lots of bits and pieces to string together. But having too many leads was far better than having none at all.

CHAPTER 5

Next morning I asked Don to meet me at Dewey's for lunch. I didn't think he'd told me everything he knew about the initials on the cryptic notes Cindy had left behind, and I wanted to question him some more. Betty dropped by the office with the list of names I'd requested, and we chatted a while about some of the people I might talk to. Then it was time to see Don.

I drove to Dewey's in silence. I couldn't think of any CD I could play that would prepare me for a meeting with Don.

He was already seated in a booth when I arrived. Dewey rushed up to me as soon as I came in the door. "Claire, did you know Don was here?" he whispered.

"Yes, I asked him to meet me."

"Oh, good. I didn't want a scene."

I gave a short laugh. "Okay, Dewey, since you don't want a scene, there won't be any. We'll be perfectly civilized, I promise. Now dig us up something from the alley so we can eat."

"You got it." Dewey practically ran back to the kitchen.

I slid into the booth and faced Don. "Hi. Thanks for meeting me."

"No problem. I'll go anywhere for lunch if a beautiful woman's buying. You said this was about the Kagel case?"

"Yes, and I promise I won't bother you about this any more after today." I pulled the paper out of my purse and laid it on the table. "You said the initials on this page meant nothing."

He nodded.

"Then how come the letters FBI leap off the page at me? Surely you contacted them."

"Yes, of course, I did. They swore they knew nothing about Cindy and had no investigations going concerning her."

"Maybe they were using her as a snitch. From what I understand, she was a handful for a while and ended up living on the street for a few months."

"Yeah, that's true. I told the fibby I talked to I was in deep doo-doo over the case and really needed some cooperation. He swore he was being straight with me. That's why I came to the conclusion the initials must have stood for her bank."

Our meals came, and we began eating. "These other initials, HC and CRF—nothing made sense with those either?"

Don shook his head while he finished chewing a bite of salad, then spoke. "I told you at the station—everything I looked at dead-ended." His brown eyes lost their warm glow. "I'm telling you everything, Claire. I'm not holding anything back.

I spoke softly, trying to calm him. "I'm sorry, Don. I know you wouldn't play games. It's just that the mom's so upset. I'd like to help her put a name and face to her daughter's killer."

He added some salt to his food. "Yeah, I know. We never meet these people at a good time."

"Did you get a feeling about any of the people you talked to, like maybe they were hiding something?"

"Just Seabold, like I told you. Never could pin anything definite on him, though."

We ate in silence for a while. "One other thing," I began, "you and I both know you have sources of info I can't tap into since I'm not on the force anymore. Did you turn up anything else that might help me?"

"No. Oh, oh." Don reached for the cell phone on his belt. "Excuse me, I'm vibrating." He held the phone to his ear. "Hello." He turned slightly away from me and lowered his voice. "Hi. Yeah, Lori, we're still on for tonight. I'm busy right now. I'll call you later, okay?" He put the phone back in its case.

My hands balled into fists in my lap. I could feel my fingernails dig into my palms. He'd moved on! I tried to sound casual. "Who's the lucky lady?"

Don blushed. "Just somebody I met at the gym. We're going to see a movie tonight." He slid to the edge of the booth. "Gotta go now. Good luck."

Good luck. That was it. Good luck. I couldn't figure out if I was more upset that Don was seeing someone else or that I hadn't found anyone first. I paid the check and slammed out of the restaurant.

During the ride to the office, I put my feelings about Don in the will-deal-with later part of my brain and concentrated on the job at hand. Bobby Spears was going to be my first target. I'd have to do some background work on him first, though. After the next few days, I'd know him as well as I know my own brother.

CHAPTER 6

I lined up an interview with one of Cindy's friends. Betty Seabold had smoothed the way for me by telling the girl I was working for her. We were going to have lunch at Dewey's, and I arrived a little early.

"Hey, Claire," Dewey greeted me, "I'm sure seeing a lot of you lately."

"That's right, and I'm meeting somebody again today," I said, putting a hand on my hip. "I've been thinking, Dewey. With all the customers I've brought you lately, you ought to start giving me a break on my bill."

"Yeah, right. That'll happen when pigs fly. Say," Dewey's voice lowered, "how'd it go with Don yesterday?"

"Okay. We had a business luncheon, that's all." I tried to sound like I was talking about the weather or something else insignificant.

Dewey's eyes bored into me, drilled into my feelings about Don. I wasn't fooling him. "Yeah, business, sure. Let me know when you're ready to order." He turned and went to another table.

I watched the people as they came through the door. Finally, I spotted a slim, black-haired woman in her twenties. She looked around as if searching for someone. I waved her over to the table.

"Carol Taylor?" I asked.

She nodded, and we shook hands. "Please, sit down." I motioned to the other side of the table.

After we went through the formalities of ordering lunch, Carol spoke. "This is kind of creepy. I never thought I'd be talking to a private detective about anything."

"I understand. I promise I'll be on my best behavior. I won't take your fingerprints or anything like that."

She smiled. "Okay. I must say I was surprised to hear from Mrs. Seabold. I thought they'd given up on trying to find whoever killed Cindy."

"The police have, but the Seabolds haven't. They've hired me to see if I can find any new information."

"I'll be glad to help in any way possible. Cindy and I grew up together. We were best friends." Carol's voice softened. "I really like Mrs. Seabold, too. I know she's been through a rough time."

I took out my notepad. "You say you and Cindy grew up together. How far back did you go?"

"We met in kindergarten. Always seemed to be in the same classes together. We had something else in common after awhile."

I looked up from my notepad. "Oh, what?"

"My dad died when I was in the second grade. Cindy lost hers a few years later. That's when we really got close. She needed help dealing with everything."

"I'm sure you were a great comfort to her. How did she handle the loss?"

"She did okay. Of course, she was upset and cried a lot for a while, but her mom and she really got close. They were like two against the world in those days."

The waitress brought our food, and I poured dressing on my salad. "I understand Betty and Cindy hit a rough patch when Betty went back to work."

Carol nodded. "Yeah, they did, but Cindy got through it. She was resentful for a while because her mom wasn't around to do stuff for her any more. But she finally realized Mrs. Seabold had to work."

So far, Carol's story jibed with Betty's. "When did Cindy meet Bobby Spears?"

"When we went to high school. Bobby was a few years older than we were. All the girls were after him."

"Why was that?"

Grinning, Carol leaned a little closer. "Bobby was a great combination. He had looks, a personality, *and* brains. Cindy was determined to reel him in, and she did."

"Sounds like my kind of girl. How'd she do it?"

Carol shifted in her seat. "Let me tell you, Cindy was no dummy. Instead of depending strictly on her looks, she decided she'd do well in school. She joined all the academic club things and got to know Bobby that way. He grew to respect her, then to love her."

I paused, thinking about Betty's sneer when she talked about Spears. "Why didn't Mrs. Seabold like Bobby?"

"I never figured out exactly what happened there. She liked him at first. Could be she got mad because he finally gave up on Cindy. I couldn't blame him though. We all gave up on her after awhile."

"Why?"

Carol shook her head. "Cindy got crazy her junior year. She stopped studying, starting hanging around with the wrong crowd. She eventually dropped out of school."

I nodded. "Mrs. Seabold told me about that. Did her new stepfather have anything to do with the changes Cindy went through?"

"Not that I know of. Cindy was really happy for her mom when she got married. Everything was going fine, then all of a sudden...." Carol raised her hands. "Poof!"

I sat with my chin cupped in my hand a moment, thinking, wondering if Carol knew more than she was telling me. "You mean she didn't confide in you at all about what was going on? I thought you two were best friends."

"I did, too, until all that happened. Believe me, it's a mystery to me why she started acting up." She smiled. "I guess that's why we need you to solve this whole thing."

"Maybe. Let's get back to Bobby. You said he gave up on Cindy."

"Yeah, he was in college trying to hang onto an academic scholarship when she came unglued. He couldn't handle his studies and her drifting in and out of his life. He finally called it quits. I heard the breakup wasn't pretty."

"What do you mean?"

"From what I heard, Cindy made a big scene—screaming and all. She threatened to mess up Bobby's life. I don't think she was serious, though."

My forearm rested on the recorder on my belt. I was glad it was on. I was going to have some interesting questions to ask Bobby Spears. "I understand Cindy was on the streets for awhile."

"Yeah." Carol waved a hand. "That was bad. She was into drugs and finally couldn't hold a job. She was on the streets for a few months, got scared, then cleaned up."

"Did she say what scared her?"

She thought a moment. "No, she was a different Cindy when I saw her again. She said something happened she didn't want to talk about, and she needed to get off the streets. She moved in with me and another friend, got a job at a food bank in West Indalia and started seeing her mom again. Everything seemed to be going so well for her, then this…." Carol's eyes teared up. She reached in her purse for a tissue.

I patted her other arm, and we sat quietly for a moment. "Anything else you want to tell me?"

Carol wiped her nose. "I can't think of anything right now."

I reached in my purse. "Here's my card. If anything at all pops into your mind, please give me a call. Even the smallest details are sometimes very important."

She stood up. "I sure will. I hope I've helped."

"You have." I motioned for the check.

Later, in the car, my fingers drummed on the steering wheel as I waited for the light to change. I felt more alive than I had in a long time. I'd had a great lunch interview with more leads popping up. What could be better? Two more questions demanded answers. What scared Cindy when she was on the street? And did Bobby Spears take Cindy's threats seriously? It was definitely time to home in on the boyfriend.

CHAPTER 7

After checking various sources, I found what Carol had said about Bobby Spears was true. He was good-looking, well liked, and bright. He'd gotten a degree in computer science and was working for a company called Computer Reasoning Factor. The business dealt with various computer solutions and services such as repair, database set-up, Web site design, and software applications. He was considered a comer.

I decided to tail him for a few days to get to know his routine, so I put on my uniform of sunglasses, sunshade, and wig of mousy brown hair. I love my red hair, but not when I'm following someone. Best not to stand out in a crowd.

His routine on workdays was predictable. He'd leave for work about eight-thirty every morning, eat at the same restaurant for lunch, and head home about five or six o'clock in the evening. The interesting thing was that home was an apartment right on the canal. Home also had another resident, his girl friend Helen Colson. Bobby'd moved on, too.

The restaurant looked like the best place to question Bobby. I decided not to make a pre-arranged appointment with him. I didn't want to give him time to think about what to say. As I was leaving my apartment to try to see him at lunchtime, my pump started beeping. I saw a Low Reservoir warning on the screen. *Great. I'd better put more insulin in my pump before I see Bobby.* I glanced at my watch. *Hope I have enough time.*

I quickly got my supplies out, loaded the reservoir, and hooked up a new infusion set. I placed the reservoir in the pump, did a prime and jabbed the needle in my abdomen. I still had some time to spare.

The pump beeped again. What now? A Low Battery alert. Better replace it now. I quickly replaced the battery. *Still within the time frame, but I've gotta move fast to make it.* I attempted to attach my pump to my clothing and pick up my notepad at the same time. Bad idea. The pad caught on the tubing, and the pump fell on the floor. *Am I ever going to get out this door?* I threw the notepad at the wall, then checked the pump. Luckily it had fallen on the carpet and seemed to be okay. I looked at the tubing. That was not okay. I saw pink fluid mixed with the insulin. In my haste to insert the needle manually, I must have hit a blood vessel. I'd have to start all over again.

I had to face it. There was no way I was going to see Bobby Spears today. And all because of a stupid insulin pump. I sat for a moment taking a few deep breaths to calm myself.

Then I did what I had to do to get back on track. As the final straw, when I monitored my blood sugar I found my anger had pushed my reading up.

A quiet meal among friends at Dewey's seemed like a good way to get back on track. I slid into my usual booth and decided to treat myself to a piece of cake with lunch. I'd had a rough morning, so I'd earned it. Cathy, a waitress who'd been with Dewey since the Flood, took my order. She gave me a stare when I ordered the chocolate cake.

"Can you have that, Claire? I thought diabetics weren't allowed to have sugar."

Great! Now a waitress is part of the diabetes police. I tightened my jaw and spoke. The words escaped through my clenched teeth and penetrated the restaurant. "Yes, Cathy, I can have cake. Today I need cake. Today I need the biggest piece of cake in the world!"

Other diners stared at me as Cathy hurried away to fill my order. I glared at them, and they quickly turned back to their meals.

Cathy was back in a few minutes sliding a plate onto the table. "I'm sorry if I upset you, Claire. I was just concerned. We all care about you in here." Her eyes pleaded with me to understand.

"I'm sorry, Cathy. It's been a bad morning. I didn't mean to take it out on you. I promise I'm careful about what I eat. I can have treats like anybody else as long as I use common sense. Now go tell Dewey to give you a raise."

After lunch, I decided to head for the hospital. I knew a diabetes support group would be meeting there. Today I needed that support.

The group was in the midst of the meeting when I arrived, but the members paused to give me a warm greeting.

Steve, the leader, got me a chair. "Haven't seen you for awhile, Claire. How's it going?"

"You just asked the wrong question. It's not going today." I sat down and went through the litany of my day's problems. Most people smiled when I got to the part about Cathy and the cake. I could tell they were remembering similar incidents in their own lives. "I think the worst thing is that everything I've done today has reminded me I have diabetes."

"That's a fact, isn't it?" asked Steve.

"Yes, but it all seems to close in on days like today."

An older man raised his hand. "You know what? As I was leaving for the meeting, I got a call from a friend who said his son was in a head-on collision. They don't expect him to make it. I got me another friend who has terminal cancer."

"So?" *What's this guy's point?*

"So—stuff happens. We have diabetes. Somebody else has cancer or whatever. It can always be worse."

The woman sitting next to him spoke. "It can always be worse, but I understand how Claire feels."

Steve turned to me. "Are you still angry that you have diabetes?"

I was silent for a moment. The question caught me by surprise. "I—I guess I am," I finally admitted. "And why not? My whole life changed after I was diagnosed. I couldn't do the work I wanted to any more. My fiancé and I broke up. My blood sugars were all over the place. Everything seemed to go wrong." I looked at everyone, knowing they'd understand. "Then I thought I was getting a handle on things. I got into a routine with my eating and exercise, got my sugar under control. But today reminded me how things can go wrong so quickly."

Steve put his hand on my shoulder. "It's okay to be angry and frustrated sometimes, but don't let those emotions take over. You need to accept the fact that you have diabetes and move on from there." The group nodded in agreement.

I stayed for the rest of the meeting and, at the end, got hugs from some of the folks. I thanked Steve for his comments and left knowing I had to get a better grip on my feelings. I flipped in a new CD and listened to the Mars cut from Holst's "Planets".

Watch out, Bobby Spears, I'm definitely coming after you tomorrow.

CHAPTER 8

The next morning I made sure the pump, and everything connected with it, was functioning perfectly. No way was I getting sidetracked today. I parked across the street from Spears' restaurant and waited for him to enter for lunch. I'd decided to use a cover story when I talked with him. Since feelings between him and the Seabolds might be running deep on both sides, I didn't want him to know I was working for Betty and Clint.

Finally he showed, and I hightailed it across the street. I walked up to his table, fake business card in hand. "Mr. Spears?"

He looked up from his menu. "Yes?"

"Hi. I'm Claire Burton, a freelance writer. I'm doing an article on Cindy Kagel's death and wondered if you could give me some information."

Spears sagged in his seat. "After they found Cindy's body, I talked to police and reporters 'til I was blue in the face. I don't feel like going over everything again."

"I can understand that, but there's a chance new leads might be uncovered if the story appears in the paper again."

Spears' face brightened. "Do you really think so?"

I was surprised by his eagerness. Would he really be happy about new leads? "It's worth a try, isn't it?" I slid into the chair across from him. Close up, Spears' beach boy good looks contrasted sharply with the business suit he was wearing.

"Yeah, I guess so." He shoved his menu aside. "What do you want to know?"

I flipped my notepad open. "I understand you and Cindy dated for awhile. How did you get to know each other?"

"We met in high school. She was a couple of years younger than me, but so intelligent. That's what attracted me to her—the fact that she was so smart for her age."

"Really." I smiled. "You're the first man I've ever heard of that liked a woman for her mind first."

Bobby laughed. "I guess that does sound funny, especially for a high school boy, but Cindy was the complete package. She was smart, pretty, and caring."

"How long did you two date?"

"We went steady until her junior year, then the bottom dropped out of everything."

"What do you mean?"

"Something happened that changed Cindy. She'd never tell me what, but it must have been something serious."

"How could you tell?"

The waitress came and got our orders. Bobby continued. "We used to see each other on a regular basis even when I went to college. But after this thing—whatever it was—happened, she'd come and go as the mood struck. I never knew when I was going to see her. I could tell she was using, too."

"What was she on?"

"I'm pretty sure it was crack. She was high a lot of times when we met."

"The change must have been hard to put up with."

"It was. I finally had to break things off with her. I couldn't stand seeing her go downhill. I couldn't keep up my grades and be her babysitter, too."

The waitress brought our lunches. I shifted my notepad and asked, "How'd she take it?"

Bobby rolled his eyes. "Very badly. She was strung out when I told her, and she went nuts. She screamed and yelled. Said she'd ruin my life."

"Wow. That must have upset you."

"Yeah, it did. Especially when she started stalking me." Bobby shook his head and winced. "It got really bad when I started seeing someone else. We'd go out, and there Cindy would be. High as a kite and yelling about how I should be with her. A couple of times she tried to get physical with us."

I put down my pad. "That surprises me. Doesn't sound like the Cindy other people have told me about."

"I know. It surprised me, too. I think it was the drugs."

"You must have had some fun dates with all that going on. How did the girl you were dating take Cindy's actions?"

"Helen? She hung in there. She can take care of herself."

"Twenty-first century woman, huh? What's her last name?"

"Colson, Helen Colson." Bobby leaned toward me. "Please don't bother her. She's been through enough, and things are good for us now. Besides, Cindy's dead. It wouldn't do any good to dredge up old memories."

I nodded, not committing one way or the other. "Did Cindy keep bothering you until she died?"

"No, she disappeared for a while, then popped up again."

"Was she still strung out?"

"No, she came to my office. Said she'd cleaned up and had a job. She came by for a professional visit. She wanted me to help her with a computer accounting system."

"Why?"

Bobby took the last bite of his lunch, then spoke. "It had to do with her job. She was working for some charitable organization—Food Bank for Indigents. She thought there was something wrong with the accounting software they had and wanted to install a new system."

"Any problems with her while she was in your office?"

Bobby hesitated. "Uh, no. No. Everything was fine. She was her old self. I was so glad she was back on track, then...." He looked down at his plate. "Then she was gone." He looked up at me, eyes moist. "I need to get back to work." He started to rise from his seat. "I don't think there's anything else I can tell you."

I held up my hand. "One more thing. Did anyone see you with Cindy in the office?"

"Yes, Callie, the receptionist." He called over his shoulder as he walked quickly to the cash register.

I was surprised by Bobby's emotions. Was he just upset because Cindy was dead or was he, maybe, feeling guilty?

I went back to the office and fired up the computer, dreading what I was going to have to do. Since I'd told Bobby I was a freelance writer, I was going to have to write a story about the murder in order to stay out of trouble with my licensing board. That blasted No Subterfuge rule tended to get in my way, and I was skating close to the edge. If I had a story all ready to go, I could always tell them I was going to submit it to the newspaper.

As I typed away, I realized writing the story was actually helping me. The leads were piling up, and I had to decide which way to go next. Eventually I'd have to go down to the less scenic part of town and find out what had scared Cindy. I'd also have to talk with Callie, the receptionist and Helen Colson, the girl friend. Lots of work to do. What to do next?

The phone rang interrupting my thoughts. Betty Seabold's voice on the other end sounded tired. "Claire, how are you coming with the case?"

"Not bad. I've got some leads I'm going to follow up. After I do, I'll call you with an update."

"Good. I can tell Clint you're getting somewhere. He's been giving me a hard time about the expenses. We're not rolling in money, you know."

"I understand, Betty. Believe me, I'm not running up the charges unnecessarily. By the way, I'm glad you called. I talked with Bobby Spears today. He seemed decent to me. Why don't you like him?"

"He was my last hope of getting Cindy straightened out before she ran away. She wouldn't talk to me any more, so I was hoping he could do something with her. It seemed to me in the end he cared more about his grades than he did her."

"I think he got frustrated with her like everyone else."

I didn't hear anything on the other end of the line. "Betty? Are you still there?"

"Yes. I was just thinking. I guess being mad with Bobby was really a mother's frustration…." She started crying.

"Betty, it's okay." I tried to soothe her.

She cleared her throat. "I know. I just miss her so much."

My heart wrenched. "I promise you, if it's the last thing I do, I'll get to the bottom of this mess. I'll find her killer."

We said our good-byes. I stared at my story for a few minutes, thinking about Betty's grief. I straightened my shoulders. Back to business. Bobby's canal apartment girl friend, Helen Colson, would be my next target.

CHAPTER 9

Before I talked with Helen, I studied the paperwork I had on her. She was in her mid-twenties and was running a gymnasium for her parents. The place used to be known as Colson's Gym before Helen began to manage it. Now it was called Firm Bodies, Inc. I gathered she was trying to appeal to the uptown crowd. It seemed to be working. The business was doing well.

The phone rang again. I gave my official Claire Burton, Investigator hello and heard my mother's voice on the other end of the line. "Claire, this is Mom."

"Hi, Mom. What's up?"

"I just wanted to remind you about dinner tonight. Please don't be late. We have a surprise for you."

Oh boy, is it Tuesday again already? "Okay. I'll be there on the dot. Are you going to give me any hints about what's going on?"

Mom giggled. "If I did that, it wouldn't be a surprise now, would it?"

I couldn't argue with logic like that. "Can you at least tell me if it's a good surprise?"

"It's a wonderful surprise, I promise you. Remember, be here at seven sharp."

"Got it, Mom. Gotta run now." As I hung up the phone, I wondered what the surprise was. Whatever it was, Mom seemed excited. I shrugged and got back to the Colson file. After reading a while longer, I decided to change into my sweats and scope out Firm Bodies, Inc. before I talked to Helen.

The gym was near the canal and had been renovated at about the same time. The glass front allowed passersby to see people inside willingly working up a sweat. As I walked in, I hoped this wasn't the gym where Don and his sweet little thing, Lori, worked out.

The place had plenty of machines and weights for self-inflicted torture. I could also see a room off to the side reserved for aerobics classes. Even though the radio blared over the PA system, the atmosphere was hushed, temple-like. People were quiet—absorbed in trying to do one more rep, defining one more muscle, pushing themselves to the limit.

"Can I help you?"

I turned at the sound of the voice. A girl at the desk was smiling at me.

"I just wanted to see what the gym was like— take a look around."

"You're welcome to have a trial workout if you'd like. Only costs five dollars."

I looked at my watch, making sure I could fit the workout in before dinner. "Sounds good." I plunked down the cash, set the pump to my exercise basal rate, and started warming up on the stationary bike. Before long I was flexing muscles on the machines like everyone else.

As I finished up, I noticed a blonde with dark roots talking with the girl at the desk. The blonde had a dark complexion and was wearing a workout suit. Apparently she was Helen Colson because she began checking the books. I decided to work out a bit longer so I could observe her. She finished her paperwork, then warmed up and came out on the floor as if she was going to challenge every weight in the room. I watched her bench press some respectable pounds. *Watch out, Claire. She could give you a run for your money.*

Finally, I decided I'd seen enough. *Better get to Mom and Dad's and find out about the big surprise.* I checked my sugar before I left to make sure my basal rate had been lowered enough for the exercise. Everything was fine, so I hopped in the car.

Mom met me at the door. "I was getting worried. It's after seven."

I looked at my watch. "I'm only ten minutes late. I got tied up."

"It's just that I'm so anxious for you to know something." Her eyes sparkled. "Wait 'til you see who's here." She pushed me gently toward the living room.

Mom was right. She did have a surprise. There on the couch sat my brother, Gene. A very attractive brunette was sitting next to him.

"Gene! What are you doing here? I thought you were working over in Parkersburg."

"I am, little sister, but I brought home someone special I wanted you all to meet." Gene and his lady friend both rose as I crossed to the couch.

"They're engaged," Mom gushed.

"Ariel." Dad came in from the kitchen. "You should have let Gene tell Claire that."

"I'm sorry. I'm so excited I couldn't keep still any longer."

I hugged both Gene and whoever his fiancée was and we all sat down. "When did this happen?"

"Last night." He grinned. "Oh, I'm being stupid. Emily, this is my sister, Claire." Emily smiled and nodded.

"Okay, Gene. I need all the details. How did you meet? How long have you known each other? And the main question, why in the world would she want to marry you?"

Everyone laughed, even Emily. Gene took Emily's hand. "You see, Emily. I told you my sister was a detective. Always asking questions." He turned to me. "You remember when I went to work for the accounting firm in Parkersburg?"

I nodded.

"I met Emily there. Her dad owns the business. He had a party for the staff one night. I took one look at her, and the rest, as they say, is history."

"Congratulations to you both. When's the big day?"

Emily took over the conversation. Weddings are a woman's business, and I could tell she was in her element. "About six months from now. There's so much to do. I'll need every minute to get ready."

We chatted about the arrangements for a while, then Emily changed the subject. "I couldn't believe it when Gene said his sister was a private detective. Sounds dangerous to me."

"It's not really. Actually it involves a lot of paperwork like Gene's job."

Emily stroked Gene's copper red hair. "I'm glad Gene's not doing that kind of work. It still sounds dangerous to me."

"If I'd been a detective, I wouldn't have met you either." His hand lifted her chin. They stared into each other's eyes for a moment, oblivious to everyone else in the room.

The rest of the evening was spent in more conversation about wedding plans, how big and successful Emily's dad's company was, and how Gene would certainly rise right to the top.

After hugs and good-byes I drove home, entered my apartment and flipped on the lights. My humble abode. A bedroom, a bath, a living room, and a dinette/kitchen area. It was so small I could practically stir soup on the stove with one hand and turn down the bed with the other hand.

I huddled on the bed. I was happy for my brother, but... The tears came. Gene had everything going for him—his good looks, the great job, the beautiful girl. I was alone. I had no fiancé, and I didn't know how long the Kagel job might last. Clint could pull the plug any minute, and I'd be back where I started. I cried for a while then dried my eyes. Enough.

There was something I needed to see. I opened the jewelry box on the dresser and pulled out the medal. Fingering the decoration, I thought about how I'd been awarded it for bravery after rescuing a little girl from an ugly hostage situation. I held it in my hand, remembering the thrill of beating the bad guys, thinking about the grateful looks on the parents' faces when I brought the little girl home. *Stop the pity party, Claire. This is what you do. This* is what you want to do, and you'll continue doing it somehow.

I took Cindy's picture from my purse. *Your parents will be the next grateful faces I see. I promise.*

CHAPTER 10

Next morning I waited in the car outside Firm
Bodies until I saw the blonde enter. I walked
in, notepad in hand, ready to gather more
information. She was at the desk talking with the
receptionist when I handed her my card.

"Hi. Helen Colson?" She smiled and nodded.
"I'm Claire Burton, a freelance writer. I'm doing a
story on the Cynthia Kagel murder, and I'm hoping
you can give me some information."

Her smile stiffened. "What makes you think I
know anything about Cindy Kagel?"

"I understand you started seeing Bobby Spears
after he broke up with Cindy. I believe you're still
seeing him."

She looked at the intently listening receptionist,
then back at me. "Step into my office."

We entered a small office off the reception area, and I started toward a chair in front of the desk.

"Don't even think about sitting down." Helen spit the words out. "I'm sick and tired of Cindy Kagel, so you're not going to be in here that long."

I plopped down anyway. "Look, I'm not here to make trouble. I talked with Bobby the other day, and he was very cooperative."

Helen frowned. "He didn't mention it."

"I explained to him that running a story right now might produce more leads." I pulled out a pen and poised it over the notepad.

She sat down at the desk, crossed her arms, and gave me a cold look. "All right. Go ahead and ask questions, but I don't see how I can be of much help."

"How did you meet Bobby?"

"I started running the gym for my parents when they began having health problems. I decided to try some newer methods of promoting the place like getting a Web site for it.

I found out you could go to the university and get a student to help set up a site." She sat back in her chair, finally starting to relax. "The school thought it would be a good deal for the students to get experience, and it was certainly a good deal for me."

"So Bobby was the student." I was glad Helen was opening up.

She smiled. "Yes, he was. As we worked more and more together, things started to click. We began dating."

"When did you find out about Cindy?"

"I could see something was upsetting Bobby. I asked him what was going on, and he told me Cindy was following him, threatening him, and making scenes."

I nodded. "That's what he told me. Did you ever see her do anything like that?"

Helen made a face. "More than once, I'm afraid."

"What did she do?"

"We'd go out to a movie, or dinner, or whatever, and there she'd be—jumping out at us, screaming, saying she'd find some way to break us up."

"That must have been pretty upsetting. How'd you handle it?"

"I tried to ignore her at first, but I finally got tired of it. She came at us one night, and I gave her a good shove. She fell backwards down a little hill. We never saw her after that."

"Guess it pays to work out at a gym."

She laughed.

I made a few notes, then looked up from my writing. "So she never contacted you or Bobby again?"

"No, thank heavens."

There was a light rap at the door. It opened and a male voice spoke.. "Hi, hon. Did I leave my softball bat here?"

I grimaced. It was Bobby Spears. *Don't think he'll be too happy to see me.*

Helen turned in her chair. "Yeah, it's right here." She picked up the bat and held it out to him.

As he took it, he noticed me. "You! What are you doing here? I told you not to bother Helen!"

Helen sprang from her chair. "What's going on, Bobby? She said she talked to you the other day, and you were very helpful."

"I was, but I told her to leave you alone." He stood there, bat in hand, glowering at me.

This is not good. Time to go, Claire. I jumped up. "Just trying to cover all the story angles," I said as I shoved past him. He was still yelling when I got to the outside door. I let out a relieved sigh, then felt like taking it back. *I don't believe what I'm seeing.* Don and some girl toy were getting out of the car in front of the gym. Apparently they did work out here.

"Claire! How's it going?" Don asked.

"Peachy, peachy keen," I said, hurrying across the street to my car.

I drove a ways, then parked, and started walking along the canal. I needed to clear my head. *Stop thinking about the Don thing and get back to the case.* While the visit to the gym may have ended badly,

I had gathered more facts which led to more questions. Helen Colson certainly had enough physical strength to drag a body anywhere. Bobby had a bat. Could either one of them have been angry enough with Cindy to hit her in the head and dispose of her body in the canal? And why hadn't Bobby told Helen he'd seen Cindy again? I also had to figure out how to see Bobby's receptionist, Callie, without his knowing. I didn't need another run-in with Batboy.

The walk along the canal did the trick. I knew how I was going to question Callie.

CHAPTER 11

Before questioning Callie, I needed to finish up my other job. I drove over to Hartville that evening, mousy brown wig on, camera at the ready. Sure enough, the winker idiot Mr. Talbott was bowling his heart out. I'm sure everyone thought I was a groupie of his as I took several pictures of his excellent bowling form.

He placed a respectable second and won five hundred dollars. I hoped it would tide him over when the workers' comp stopped, and he lost his job.

The next day, I dropped the report and pictures by the office of the lawyer who'd hired me.

"Here you go, Flint." I pushed the papers across the desk. "I think this'll make your client happy."

He sifted through the file's contents. "Looks good, Claire! I'll pay you as soon as I get my fee."

I left, hoping that would be sooner rather than later. Clint could always decide the investigation wasn't worth it and pull the plug on me. Oh well, on to receptionist Callie.

I put my wig back on and headed to Computer Reasoning Factor. A glance at my watch told me Bobby should be nicely settled in his office. I entered the one-story stucco building.

As I opened the door, a white-haired woman sitting at the reception desk greeted me. "May I help you?" she asked.

"Yes, I'm working for the building manager. He asked me to stop by and make sure everything's working properly." Okay, I was going against the No Subterfuge rule. So sue me.

"Everything's fine as far as I know."

"Climate controls, cleaning staff, everything else good for you?"

"Yes, things seem to be working fine."

"Okay, guess that does it." I started toward the door then turned back. "Say, you folks do computer work here, don't you?"

"Yes. We have solutions for most computer problems you might encounter." Callie reached for brochures.

"My cousin needs someone to design a Web site for him. Could your people take care of that?"

"Why, yes. We have several very capable people—Mr. Lichten, Ms. Jacobsen, Mr. Spears."

I took the brochures. "Spears, huh. We were asking around, and someone else mentioned his name. Must be good."

"He's the best." She handed me Bobby's business card.

I studied it. "Spears, Bobby Spears. Why does that name sound familiar?" I paused as if deep in thought. "Isn't he the guy who was mixed up with that Kagel girl?"

Callie studied me for a moment. "I guess you're all right. You don't have red hair."

"What's that supposed to mean?"

"Mr. Spears told me to be on the lookout for some writer who's poking around about Cindy Kagel. He told me not to talk to her. He said she was a redhead, though."

I laughed. "Well, I'm glad I passed that test. I guess that means he was mixed up with the Kagel girl."

"Yes," she agreed, "he was."

"It was awful what happened to her."

"Yes, it was a real shame. I saw her right here in the office." The phone rang, and Callie did her receptionist duty. She looked up after writing a message. "I think that's probably all I should say to you. I don't want to get into trouble with Mr. Spears."

"I understand." I put my hand on the doorknob, then turned back again. "I just had a thought. You might have been one of the last people to see Cindy Kagel alive. What was she like?"

Callie thought a moment. She motioned me to come closer and spoke softly. "Very nice. She came for some computer help. Of course she wanted to see Mr. Spears."

"I guess so, since they were dating."

"Oh no, Mr. Spears had another girl friend at that time."

"And that didn't bother Cindy?"

"It didn't seem to when she came in, but when she left…." Callie shook her head.

"What happened?"

Callie drew back. "Maybe I shouldn't say."

"Oh, come on. I promise it'll be just between us girls."

Callie drew close again, obviously unable to resist the temptation to spill some office gossip. "Like I said, she went into the office all friendly and everything, but she came out crying."

"Really. Could you figure out why?"

"No. Mr. Spears came to the door and called out to her, but she kept going."

"I guess we'll never know now what happened."

"Guess not."

I opened the door. "Thank you. You've been a big help. I'll turn in my report to the building manager."

I waited until I got in the car before I took off the wig. Mr. Spears was going to have to answer a few more questions over another lunch. I might give him indigestion, but I had to know why Cindy was crying when she left his office.

I glanced at my watch and saw I had time for an errand. After a short drive, I pulled up to the pharmacy. Betty Seabold had given me a check for my first week's work. I could splurge on insulin. Joe, the pharmacist, was at the counter waiting on a customer when I walked up. His pressed white jacket was so starched he couldn't have slouched if he wanted to.

"Hi, Claire. Be right with you."

"Sure, Joe. Take your time."

He finished with the customer, then went to the refrigerator in the pharmacy and pulled out my insulin order. "Hey, I got a great new blood glucose monitor. It's got a lot of bells and whistles. I thought you might be interested. Want to see it?"

I had a few minutes, so I agreed. Joe demonstrated all the fancy features, then asked, "What do you think? Does it look like something you can use?"

"Will it do the dishes?"

He laughed. "No, sorry, we're not there yet."

"I guess I'll wait. I'm sure they'll add that feature at some point."

Joe called out for me to have a nice day as I left. I took the insulin to the office and headed for Bobby's restaurant.

He was there studying the menu when I walked up to the table. "Hi, Bobby."

He looked up. His face reddened when he recognized me. "You! I thought you got the picture at the gym." He slammed the menu on the table. "I don't want to talk to you, and I don't want you talking to Helen or anyone else about Cindy. It's all too painful."

I sat down, hoping he hadn't brought the bat to lunch with him.

He looked around. "Do I have to call someone to remove you?"

"Simmer down," I said, trying to soothe him. "Please, hear me out. I'm not really a writer."

"What! Who are you then?"

"My name is Claire Burton as I said, but I'm a private investigator. The Seabolds hired me to look into Cindy's case because the police never solved her murder. I didn't know how you felt about Betty and Clint. That's why I came up with the writer cover story."

He frowned for a moment. Then his face softened, and he leaned back in his seat. "That makes sense. I know Betty was mad at me for giving up on Cindy. She thought I could get through to her, but nobody could at the time we broke up."

"I need to ask you a few more questions, okay?"

He pursed his lips and thought a moment. "What more could you possible need to ask? You've already questioned Helen and me once."

"I know, but some things Helen said made me curious." I could tell by his frown he wasn't happy with me. "I promise—just a few more questions.

Bobby sighed. "Okay, go ahead."

"When I talked to Helen, she said she had to get physical with Cindy at one point."

"That's true. But it was only after Cindy hounded us time and time again. Did Helen tell you Cindy scratched her up pretty good one time?"

I raised an eyebrow. "No. Is that when she shoved Cindy down the little hill?"

"No. I'd told Helen that Cindy was troubled, so she was trying to be patient. She walked away when Cindy attacked her, but she told me later she wasn't going to take any more."

"What happened when Cindy visited you at work? I understand she left your office crying. Why was that?"

His eyes widened. I'd caught him in a lie, and he knew it. Unfortunately the waiter came at that moment, so Bobby was able to collect his thoughts while we ordered lunch. He carefully unfolded his napkin, placed it on his lap, and began speaking. "After Cindy and I were finished talking about the accounting software, she started making advances."

"What do you mean?"

"You know. She wanted us to get back together. She said she'd turned her life around, and she wanted me to give our relationship another chance."

"What did you say to that?"

"I said it was too late. I was in love with Helen, and we were committed to each other."

"Did Cindy make a scene?"

He shook his head. "Not really. She did start crying. I tried to comfort her, but she shook me off and left."

I decided to zero in on another little fact Bobby'd kept quiet. "Helen told me you two never saw Cindy again after the night she shoved her. Why didn't you tell her about the meeting in your office?"

"I didn't want to upset her. She'd already had more than enough of Cindy."

"Were you afraid she'd get violent with Cindy?"

He slapped his napkin on the table. "That's it. You may be trying to help the Seabolds, but I've had enough of your ridiculous questions. Get out!"

Heads turned at the sound of Bobby's voice, and the maitre d' started walking in our direction. I decided it was time to leave. I didn't like the food anyway.

As I drove back to the office, I wondered what else Bobby had lied about or tried to cover up.

CHAPTER 12

The weather next morning was bright and sunny. It looked like a good day to go to a part of town that wouldn't be featured on any tourist brochure. I was going there to try to find an old friend of mine and also look over the last place Cindy Kagel worked before her murder.

As I dressed, I added another accessory to my wardrobe—the oh so feminine, Lady Smith hand-gun. I enjoyed the feel of cold steel whenever I went to West Indalia. After I finished dressing, I had to laugh. I had an insulin pump, a tape recorder, and a holstered gun attached to my body. *Is there anything else you'd like to wear, Claire? Perhaps some grenades or a machete?* I shrugged. Tools of the trade.

I exited my apartment, headed west, and entered territory I'd known like the back of my hand while I was on the force. My hometown is a nice moderate-sized midwestern town, but it has its ugly side. As I drove, the streets became narrower and dirtier. So-called homes ranged from overcrowded, rat-infested apartment buildings to cardboard boxes.

Little Billy, a contact I used to use, wasn't in his favorite alley. It was probably too early for him to be up.

Might as well check out the facility where Cindy worked at the time she was murdered. I found an old brick two-story, graffiti-decorated building with a large barred window next to the entrance. The sign—Food Bank for Indigents—was barely visible through the grating. A few of the neighborhood regulars shuffled in the facility door as I got out of the car. I hoped my Saturn would still have its engine when I finished here.

Inside, the first floor looked to be mostly a warehouse with rows of canned food cartons sitting on metal racks about six feet high. There were some bins with fruits and vegetables. My nose wrinkled at the pungent odor of cabbage. Locker-style refrigerators held eggs. Freezers were also part of the equipment, but their shelves were empty at the moment. A thin fortyish woman wearing jeans and a T-shirt stood behind a table stacked with bulging paper bags. She was handing out daily rations to the folks who'd come in. She scrutinized me when I approached. I'm sure I didn't look like her usual client.

"Can I help you?"

"Yes," I replied. "I've heard about the good work you folks do, and I wanted to find out more about what goes on here."

Her mouth curved up in a tiny smile. "How badly do you want to find out?"

"Why?"

"Because the main rush for this food will start in about fifteen minutes, and my volunteer hasn't shown up. I could sure use some help."

"Okay. Count me in."

"My name's Irene, by the way." We shook hands and began opening boxes and bagging up canned goods and fresh foods. Then people started pouring in. Some, obviously, lived on the streets or in cars. Others from the apartments brought small children with them. They all seemed grateful for the supplies.

At last the crowd thinned. "Whew," said Irene, brushing some ash blonde hair back from her forehead, "glad that's over for today."

"You weren't kidding about the rush. I wouldn't have believed it if I hadn't seen it."

She smiled. "I can't thank you enough. If you're still interested in our work, I think you should meet our director, Mr. Carpenter."

I chuckled. "You haven't discouraged me yet. I'd be happy to meet him."

We climbed a narrow flight of steps to the offices on the second floor. Irene ushered me into Mr. Carpenter's office. A slight man with sallow complexion and thinning hair sat at the desk. He loosened his tie as he spoke sharply into the phone.

"I'm doing the best I can with the money you're giving me. You're not even thinking about the children down here. ... Yes, we'll definitely talk about that. Good-bye." He looked up, disgust plain on his face.

"City Hall again?" Irene asked.

"Need you ask? I'm getting fed up with them expecting miracles on the crumbs they give us from the city budget. They don't even care about the kids we try to help." He glanced at me. "Forgive me, I didn't mean to inflict city politics on you."

Irene gestured at me. "This lady saved my life today. She came by to see what we do here and stayed to help hand out food." She put her hand to her mouth. "I'm sorry. I didn't even ask your name."

"I'm Claire."

Mr. Carpenter extended his hand. "Harold Carpenter. Glad to meet you. Please sit down."

I sat on a wooden chair in front of Harold Carpenter's metal desk. A clutter of paperwork covered the desktop, and a computer terminal sat on a small table behind it.

Irene stood in the open doorway. "I'll go back downstairs now and take care of the stragglers. Hope to see you again, Claire."

I smiled and turned back to Carpenter. "Thanks so much for helping Irene," he said. "Sometimes our volunteers don't show up, then she's inundated." His elbow nudged a stack of reports. He grabbed them quickly to prevent a cascade of paper from hitting the floor. He looked back at me. "By the way, would you be interested in becoming a volunteer?"

I could see the computer screen behind him. Looked like he'd been entering some figures into an accounting program. Maybe Cindy'd worked with the program. The stacks of paperwork alone would be worth investigating. The computer was an added bonus. Volunteering here would be a perfect opportunity to check the place out.

"I think so." I didn't want to appear too anxious. "What kind of schedule would I have to follow?"

Harold grinned. "Any schedule you want to. Our motto here is 'beggars can't be choosers.'"

"Okay, I'll give it a whirl." I got up from the chair. "I'll tell Irene when I can work."

"Great! And thanks for today." Carpenter turned back to the computer screen as I left the office.

Mercifully, when I got to my car, the windows were still intact and no spray paint was visible on the doors. I drove around a while looking for Little

Billy, then gave up for the day. I could always try again tomorrow.

My phone was ringing as I entered the office. "Hi, Claire. It's Emily."

I paused for a moment. *Emily. Emily. Why was that name so familiar? Oh, yeah. My brother's fiancée. Of course.* "Hi, Emily. How are you?"

"I'm fine. Claire, I know this call is out of the blue, but I was wondering if we could get together for dinner tonight. I'd like to get to know you better."

"Tonight, let's see, tonight." I pretended to flip through a busy social calendar. Emily seemed like a nice enough person. Guess it wouldn't hurt to visit with her for a while. "Looks good. Let's do it."

We made arrangements to meet at Bobby Spears' favorite restaurant. It was upscale, so I thought it would appeal to Emily. And Bobby didn't usually eat his dinner there. I went home and looked through the clothes in my closet. I had a feeling my usual garb of dark pantsuit and light jersey wouldn't be appropriate, so I fished out a dress that was hanging in the back. It was a basic, black A-line. Should be perfect for the occasion after I dressed it up with a little jewelry.

I popped my pump in my bra, finished dressing, and headed out.

The restaurant seemed less accessible at night than when I'd seen Bobby for lunch. A pedestal for the valet parking crew stood to the side of the big oak and glass doors. Of course, a doorman was there also to open those big doors for diners.

After entering, I looked around for Emily. She hadn't arrived yet, so I scanned the tables to see if perhaps Bobby and Helen were enjoying dinner there tonight. I felt a little disappointed when I didn't spot them. It would have been fun to watch their reaction at seeing me again. I was glad, however, that a different maitre d' was on duty tonight.

"Claire. There you are." Emily patted me on the shoulder. "Let's eat. I'm starved."

The hostess showed us to a table. I noticed there was more crystal and silverware on the table than at lunchtime. I'd have to watch my manners tonight.

After ordering, we began chatting about the wedding plans. Emily seemed to have everything under control. When our dinner came, we munched away for a while. "Gene is so proud of you," she said smiling.

"Really?" That genuinely surprised me.

"Oh, yes. He told me about all your adventures when you were a policewoman, and how you picked yourself up and started your own agency after you found out you had diabetes."

"Well, you know the saying. 'You do what you gotta do.'"

"It still seems so dangerous to me." She chewed a bite of salad, then asked, "What made you want to go into law enforcement anyway?"

I put my fork down and stared at nothing—stared at my past.

"I'm sorry." Emily frowned. "I didn't mean to upset you."

"It's okay." I shook my head slightly to clear away the unpleasant memory. "I haven't thought about it for a while, that's all."

"Please, don't answer my question if you don't want to."

"You'll be part of the family soon, Emily. You might as well hear it now. I'm surprised Gene didn't tell you already."

"He said an incident with your grandfather had something to do with it, but he wasn't clear about all the details."

"Our granddad lived with us when we were growing up." I smiled when I remembered the tall, gray-bearded old man whom I'd loved so much. "He was such a gentle old guy. He was my buddy, and he had a wonderful habit. He spoiled his granddaughter."

Emily laughed. "Oh yeah? How?"

"He'd take me to the drugstore to buy us treats every once in a while. I, of course, thought it was great, except for one day."

"What happened?"

Other diners' conversation buzzed in my ears as I thought back to that day. They were probably discussing what they bought at the grocery today or something equally as trivial while I was about to reveal an occurrence that had changed my life. "We—we were at the candy counter looking at goodies when two punks came in. One of them pulled a gun and proceeded to stick up the place."

Emily put her hand to her mouth. "How awful! What did you do?"

"I froze, but Granddad was brave. He pushed me behind him so nobody could see me. On the way out, the idiot with the gun shot it into the air a couple of times." I felt my jaw tense, and I tried to relax. The old feelings of helplessness and fear that I tried to keep buried started to surface. "I can still hear the noise of the gun and the jerks' laughter as they left the store."

"That must have really scared you. At least you didn't get hurt."

"No, I didn't, but Granddad did get hurt in a way."

"How? Did a bullet hit him?"

"No. When I came out from behind him, I could see that he'd wet his pants. I was embarrassed for him, and he could see that in my face." I teared up. "I'll never forget how ashamed he looked."

Emily shook her head. "It must have been so hard for him." She took my hand. "And for you."

I blinked back the tears. I wasn't going to go all weepy in front of Emily. "I found out later that, since he was old, he didn't have good control of his bladder. The robbery was enough to make him have an accident." I wiped my nose with a tissue and spoke firmly. "I decided two things that day. Number one—I would never again freeze in a situation like that. Number two—I'd get the bad guys so nobody else would go through what Granddad and I did."

"Were you able to go in that store again?"

"Yeah, we went with no problem, but things were never the same between Granddad and me. I don't think he could get that look he saw on my face out of his mind."

"What a shame." Emily stroked my hand and gave me the pity look. I knew she was trying to be nice, but I've always hated that look.

"You know what," I looked at my watch and gathered my purse. "I really have to get going. Got a lot to do with this case." As I got up to leave, my purse knocked over a glass of water.

Emily started mopping up. "Go ahead, Claire. I'll take care of this."

I hustled the valet for my car and headed home. I felt guilty leaving the way I had, but the evening had brought up some painful memories—memories I'd always had trouble dealing with. Emily's look had also made me understand what the look on my face had meant to my grandfather. How it must have hurt him. Someday I'd have to find the time to explain my hasty departure to her.

CHAPTER 13

I went back to West Indalia the next day to volunteer at the food bank. I decided to make this a true volunteer effort and not charge the Seabolds for my time. Maybe I'd uncover some clues, maybe not. But I knew Betty and Clint were in a financial bind and could use a break on billing.

As we worked, Irene told me about the operation. She and Harold were the only paid staff at the food bank. They relied heavily on volunteers to stock shelves when deliveries came in and to make up the food packages for their clients. I told her I'd help out several times a week at the facility. That way Harold and Irene would get to know me and feel comfortable around me. Comfortable people often let their guards down and talk freely. I needed to know what they thought about Cindy. I also needed to know if they could fill in any of the blanks about her life.

I heard a truck pull up outside. Irene laughed. "This is your lucky day, Claire. You can help unload the truck." She handed me a dolly, took one herself, and headed toward the loading dock. The truck had brought donations of canned goods from a local supermarket chain. We began stacking cases of food on the dollies and rolling them back into the food bank. Harold came down from his office when he heard the commotion.

He began taking the boxes off the dollies and placing them on the metal shelving. I was surprised at the ease with which this slightly built man lifted the cartons up.

"Hey, Carpenter, very impressive." I laughed.

"What do you mean?" he asked.

"You're lifting those boxes like they don't weigh anything. I thought you were just an office type."

He smiled. "I've had to develop some arm strength. Most of the volunteers here are women. Can't expect them to heave stuff like this around."

As I handed him a carton, it caught on my insulin pump, dislodging the case somewhat. Harold saw me re-clip it to my waistband.

"You might want to think about taking off your cell phone or pager or whatever that is while we're unloading," said Harold.

"No way. This is an insulin pump. If I take it off, I'm in serious trouble."

"Oh yeah? You're diabetic?"

"Yes, for a while now."

"I've heard about insulin pumps. How does it work?"

"It's connected to a tube that goes in my body. The pump lets out a little insulin every few minutes all day long. That's known as the basal rate. When I eat a meal, I punch in the extra amount of insulin it'll take to cover the meal. That's called the bolus."

"Huh. That's interesting. So what happens if your pump gets disconnected?"

"Since I have diabetes and can't make enough of my own insulin any more, my blood sugar would go sky high. I'd be in a world of hurt. I do carry emergency supplies, though, to take care of any problems that might occur."

"That's good." Harold turned back to the boxes. "You should still be careful when unloading things, though. We don't want you to have to use those supplies."

We finished bringing in the rest of the shipment, and Harold arranged everything on the shelves. He moved the higher boxes around with a two by four so everything would fit.

I decided to take a break after everything was tucked away. I walked out in the alley, looked across the street, and there he was. Little Billy.

I'd often used Little Billy as a source when I was a cop. He was a small time drug dealer who knew a lot about West Indalia and the less-desirable citizens who live there. He stood about six feet six and was so thin he could've entered my office through the mail slot. I saw he was dressed in his usual uniform—low hanging, baggy pants and loose T-shirt. Looked like he was conducting some business. He handed a teenager a small package, and the kid handed him some greenbacks.

"Hey, Little Billy," I shouted. The tall black man turned at the sound of my voice, dreadlocks whirling around his head. The kid took off, and Little Billy crouched, ready to bolt, too, until he saw it was me. I crossed the street.

"Hey, Claire. Whatchu be scarin' me for?"

"Long time, no see, Billy. Nice to know private enterprise is still alive and well down here."

"You ain't gonna turn me in, are ya?"

"Not if you play nice."

"Whatchu be doin' down here anyway? I heard you weren't a cop no more."

I nodded. "That's true, but I missed you so much, I had to come see you again."

"Yeah, right. This ain't exactly Disneyland down here. Come on, why're you here?"

"I'm doing my civic duty." I pointed to the food bank. "I'm volunteering down here a couple of times a week."

"That's real touchin'." Billy looked up the street. "There's somebody I gotta meet now." He started to walk away. "See ya around, Claire."

"Wait a minute, Billy. I want to ask you some questions."

He turned back, a smart-mouth look on his face. "I don't gotta talk to you. You said yerself you're not a cop no more."

I reached in my purse. Billy's eyes widened, and he stepped back. "You ain't goin' fer a gun, are ya?"

"Ease up, Billy." I laughed. "There's a president I'd like you to meet."

"President?"

I withdrew a fifty-dollar bill. "Yeah. I heard President Grant was one of your favorites."

Billy relaxed and smiled. "He is." He grabbed the money from my hand. "Whatchu wanna know?"

"Gee, Billy, you really do want to talk to me. That makes me feel all warm and fuzzy inside." I went back in my purse and took out Cindy's picture. "Ever see her before?"

He studied the photo for a moment. "Yeah. She used ta work at the food bank. Nice kid. Whatever happened to 'er?"

"You heard about the floater in the canal?"

"That was her?" His face grew serious. "Never knew 'er name. She jus' want me ta call her C. K."

"Was she ever a customer?"

"Yeah, she was fer a time. Didn't have much of a habit. A little bit a' crack went a long way with her."

"I heard something happened down here that scared her. Would you, by any chance, know what it was?"

"As a matter a' fact I would. She bought a dime bag from me one night, hung around, and we started talkin', then some old dude came up the street."

"Did she know him?"

"Seemed to. She pulled me around the corner into the alley."

"Did he see you and Cindy?"

Billy laughed. "Naw, he was busy doin' other things."

"What other things?"

"He was checkin' out the merchandise—lookin' at the ladies, if ya know what I mean." Billy snickered.

"Yeah, I know what you mean. What happened after you went in the alley?"

"C. K., she peeked around the corner and watched him fer a while. Kept sayin' 'I don't believe what he's doin'."

"How long did you watch him?"

"Wasn't too long. He was quick at makin' up his mind. Chose one a' the ladies and was headed off ta the car, then he got distracted."

"How?"

"Some dumb alley cat tipped over a trash can. The guy heard the noise, looked over at us, saw C. K., and split."

"What did she do?"

"She was real upset about the whole thing. Said she had to get off the street. Next time I saw her, she was workin' over at the food bank."

"Can you tell me what the man looked like?"

Billy thought for a moment. "As I recall he was pretty ordinary lookin'. Middle-aged. Chunky dude. There's one thing I'll never forget, though."

"What was that?"

"He had the coldest gray eyes I ever saw—like lookin' at ice."

Gray eyes. Cold as ice. And Cindy knew the man. It had to be Clint Seabold. Sounded like Don's hunch about him was right. "Thanks, Billy. You've been a big help. Now get back to your sales job."

"Hang loose, Claire," he called out as he loped down the street.

It was hard to concentrate when I went back to work at the food bank. My mind kept going over the things Billy'd told me. I suspected Cindy was upset with Clint about something more than his looking for a prostitute, but what? And I remembered my visit to the Seabolds' house. Clint had wanted to tell me something about Cindy, but Betty had interrupted us.

I was hot to question Clint about a lot of things, but I knew I'd better be well prepared for a session with him. I'd have to do a little spadework first.

CHAPTER 14

I asked one of Betty Seabold's relatives, a cousin named Celia, to meet me at Dewey's the next day to talk about Betty's family reunion. The reunion had taken place around the time of Cindy's death. I wanted to know if good old Cousin Celia had seen anything peculiar. I also remembered the look on Betty's face when Clint said they'd been together the whole time. Would Celia verify that fact or not?

The lunch crowd was beginning to filter in when I got to Dewey's. He looked up and smiled when he saw me.

"You again?" he called. "Can't we get rid of you?"

"I'm a glutton for punishment," I yelled back.

Other patrons chuckled.

"What's the road kill special today?" I asked as Dewey walked toward me.

"I got a delicious chef's salad, and for you, I'll add something special—some nice chunks of dried skunk." He led me to a table where a woman of about Betty's age sat. "This lady's been asking for you. Don't ask me why. I wouldn't be seen in public with you."

The gray-haired woman dressed in a black pillbox hat and gray silk print dress looked at Dewey, then me. "Is everything all right?" she asked, eyes wide.

I laughed. "Everything's fine. We carry on like this all the time." She relaxed, and we ordered lunch.

We got acquainted as our meals were being prepared. I found out Celia was a favorite relative of Betty's and had been supportive during Cindy's wild period and subsequent death.

"What a shame it was. Cindy's death hit Betty very hard, of course." Celia's eyes moistened.

"How did Clint take it?"

"How does Clint take anything? He never lets his emotions show." Celia's mouth curled in disgust. "You'd have thought one of their pets died rather than a daughter."

"I wanted to talk to you about the family reunion. How did it go?"

Celia brightened. "We had so much fun. It was wonderful to see the family all together."

Cathy, the waitress, brought our food. I poked at the salad. "Did you take out the dried skunk?" Cathy laughed, but Celia got wide-eyed again.

"It's okay." I gave her hand a reassuring pat. "Just another joke. Please, tell me more about the reunion."

Celia gave me the run-down on all the activities the family participated in during the gathering. She even showed me pictures. Clint and Betty were together in every one of the photos.

I handed her back the prints. "Clint and Betty must have worked very hard on the reunion."

"They did," she agreed.

"I was interested in one part of the festivities in particular. Tell me about the boat trip you all went on."

"Well, as they probably told you, we were going to ride up the canal in paddle boats. I'm a little old for that, but I wanted to watch so I sat near the boat landing. Betty went to one end of the canal to make sure people didn't get tired paddling, and Clint stayed at the other end to help people get in and out of the boats."

"So they weren't together at that point."

"No, they couldn't have been."

"Did you see Clint the whole time?"

"You know, that was the funny part. He disappeared for a while. One minute he was there, the next minute he was gone. Nobody could find him."

"What happened then?"

"One of my nephews took over helping people. Then, all of a sudden, Clint was back."

"Did he say where he'd been?"

"No, he didn't. He just started working the boats again."

"About how long was he gone?"

Celia's brow furrowed as she thought. "I'd say a good hour."

We finished eating. I thanked Celia for her time and headed back to the office. The noose was tightening around Clint, but I needed to talk to Betty again. It was time for her to pay on her account anyway, so I asked her to come by the office for a report.

I felt a little guilty when I put the fifty dollars I'd given to Little Billy down on the expense sheet. It was under the category "Pay Informant", but in truth I'd given fifty dollars to a weasel to get information that might put Betty's husband in jail.

A little later I heard the door open. My heart lurched when I saw Betty. Her smile said she was hoping for news about who might have killed Cindy. Was I about to shatter her life even more?

I ushered her into the office and told her I was checking into Cindy's activities at the food bank. I didn't mention Little Billy. Then I brought the discussion around to the reunion. "I had lunch with Celia today. She was telling me about the reunion."

"That's one of the bright memories I hang on to." She choked and wiped away a tear.

"Celia told me Clint left the boat landing for a while. Do you happen to know where he went?"

Betty's face froze. "Why—why do you ask?"

"I think you know why I'm asking." I spoke firmly. "Betty, do you want me to find Cindy's killer or not?"

"Of course, I do." Her eyes flashed. "What kind of question is that?"

"Then you've got to be completely up front with me." We stared, eyeball to eyeball, over the desk. "I think you know Clint wasn't at the boat landing the whole time. Why did you lie about it?"

She nodded, her face pale. "Because I was afraid. You're right. Clint wasn't there the whole time. People were coming up to my end of the canal asking where Clint was. I didn't know, and, at the time, it didn't seem important."

"What about when they found Cindy, and the police began asking questions?"

"I wondered why Clint said we were together all the time. It scared me, so I asked him. He said he'd gone to get some drinks for the relatives. They were getting hot and thirsty. He said it would be better just to say we were together the whole time so we wouldn't waste the officers' time."

How considerate. I softened my tone. "I can see where that would make sense. We can clear this up in a hurry. I'll swing by and ask Clint what store he went to. Then that puzzle square will be filled in."

Betty relaxed in her chair. "That probably would be best. Clint's out of town right now, though. You know we own Highland Carving. He went to a trade show to check out some new items for the store."

I was still concerned about Betty's lie. "Is there anything else you're keeping from me?" I asked.

"No, I swear." Betty spoke firmly. "I'm sorry for not telling you about Clint, but I've told you everything else I know.

"Okay. I'll catch Clint when he gets back. No hurry. I don't think you even need to bother him about our session today. Like I said, it's just another square to fill in."

I found out when Clint would be back in town then showed Betty to the door. I hoped I'd been casual enough with her. I didn't want her tipping off Clint. I wanted him right where I could find him.

CHAPTER 15

To kill time until Clint got back, I decided to spend more time at the food bank. I found I liked volunteering. I especially enjoyed getting to know the kids. Harold's enthusiasm about helping the children of the area was catching. As Irene and I were handing out sacks of food one morning, a little girl tugged at Irene's jeans.

"Miss Irene, is Miss Cindy ever coming back?"

"Oh, honey." Irene put her arm around the girl's shoulder. "Claire, can you handle this by yourself for a minute. I need to talk to Kim."

She took Kim off to the side. I could see them out of the corner of my eye as I continued handing out groceries. They talked for a moment, and Kim started crying. Irene comforted her until she settled down. She came back to the table.

"What was that all about?" I asked.

"Tell you later."

Finally the morning rush died down, and we headed to the break area with its folding chairs and coffeepot. Irene handed me a cup of coffee, and we spent a few minutes in idle chitchat. When I thought the time was right, I asked a question.

"I'm curious, Irene. Who's this Cindy that Kim was asking about? I don't know any volunteer named Cindy."

Irene put her coffee down. "It's so sad. You remember the girl they found in the canal?"

I nodded.

"She used to be an employee here."

"Really?" I paused, pretending to think. "Oh yeah, I do seem to remember her name was Cindy. Cindy Kagel, wasn't it?"

"Yes. Kim got quite attached to her while Cindy was with us. Even after all this time, she still asks about Cindy. I keep trying to explain she's never coming back. Unfortunately, Kim's mentally retarded and doesn't understand."

"What did Cindy do here?"

"Pretty much what you do. It was great having her. Volunteers come and go, but I always knew I could depend on Cindy. Paid employees do show up."

"I didn't realize you ever had another employee. I thought money was tight."

"It is," Irene agreed. "After Cindy died, I asked Harold if we were going to replace her. He said we couldn't. The city'd cut the budget."

"Wow. That was a double whammy for you then—losing Cindy and the money about the same time."

Irene got another cup of coffee. "Tell me about it. I especially appreciated Cindy when she kept Harold out of the computer."

"Why?" I grinned. "Is he one of those guys who hits the wrong key all the time?"

"You got it." Irene sipped her coffee. "Harold and I were very surprised at Cindy's accounting skill—her being so young and all—but we took advantage of it. Cindy would go up to Harold's office and enter all the figures. The budget reports would be perfect."

"I thought Harold did the bookkeeping. When we were in his office the first time, I saw the accounting software up on the screen. I assumed that was part of his job."

"Oh, no. I'm the one who does it now. I'm glad you told me you saw that program on his screen. Means I'm probably in for a hassle at the end of the month." She grimaced. "Guess we'd better get back to work now."

We headed back to the food area. "Did Harold ever mess up Cindy's work?"

"Yes. I'd pass by the office, and Cindy'd be in there looking at the screen and shaking her head. I'd say, 'Harold struck again', and she'd laugh."

"Couldn't you just ask him to stay out of the program?"

"We tried, but he said he was in charge of the food bank, and he had to check figures sometimes. We couldn't argue with that." We began handing out sacks to the stragglers. "He said he'd try to be careful, but he never is."

We worked a bit longer, then Irene looked at her watch. "Time for lunch."

I headed toward the door.

"You know what, Claire?" she called after me. "Forget about what I said about Harold. He's so dedicated to this place. I can understand why he needs to see the financials. I shouldn't gripe about him."

I left and started up the street. *Oh boy.* I saw those broad shoulders and dark hair and knew I'd better head in the opposite direction.

"Claire! Wait up!"

He'd seen me. I stopped and turned. "Hi, Don. Fancy meeting you here."

"I thought I'd come down to the garden spot of Indalia and hang out."

"Yeah, sure." I smiled and looked around. "The resorts are here somewhere." I turned back to him. "What's really happening?"

"What you might expect. Somebody got murdered down here last night."

"Somebody got killed down here? Imagine that." The banter felt good. There was no tension between us.

"Yeah, big surprise. What are you doing here, by the way?"

I pointed toward the food bank. "I'm volunteering there now."

"That's great. How's the Kagel case going?"

"I've got some leads."

"Good. Let me know sometime how it's going." He turned. "I'd better head back to the station now." He started to walk away then, turned back. "Hey, you might want to check with Jim Thomas's agency if you need extra work. I had a drink with him the other night, and he was complaining about how he didn't like to do cheating spouses cases. Who knows? He might have one for you."

"Thanks. I appreciate that." Then I blurted it out. "How's Lori?" *That was really stupid, Claire.* Nothing like bringing up the other woman.

"She's fine," he said over his shoulder as he hiked up the street.

So much for banter. I headed in the other direction for lunch. Maybe I could also find a book on how to talk to ex-fiancés.

When I got back from lunch, Irene was in Harold's office frowning at the computer. "Harold struck again?" I asked.

She groaned. "He struck hard this time. Everything's all messed up."

"Hey, I just had a thought. My brother's an accountant. Maybe he can help straighten the books up. Who knows? Could be all you need is a new accounting program. Gene'll know about that stuff."

"It would be great if you could have him look over this jumble." Irene punched a few keys, and the printer started spitting out a report. "Here's the balance sheet for this month." She handed me some papers. "See if he can make any sense of it."

"Do you need me any more today?"

"No."

"Then I think I'll head over there right now."

"Thanks for all your help, Claire. See you later." Irene waved. She looked at the computer screen again and went back to frown mode.

I enjoyed the short drive over to Parkersburg. It was nice to get out of the city. I relished looking at the fields of blue, white and gold wild flowers—like splashes of paint in the bright green of the spring grass. I rolled down the window and breathed in the clean air. It was just the tonic I needed.

My brother's office was in an industrial park— one of those glass-fronted buildings that say 'look at us, we're working.'

The receptionist said, "Give me a moment. I'll see if Mr. Burton is busy." She hustled away.

Mr. Burton. Give me a break.

Gene came out with the receptionist. "Claire! What brings you here?"

"Official business, Gene. I need you to help me unravel some accounts."

"Sure. Come in my office." He led me into a room that housed a metal desk, some bookshelves, filing cabinets, and all the computer gear you could imagine.

I handed him Irene's report, explained the problem, and told him what I knew of accounting procedure at the food bank.

"I'll be glad to look this over for you." His face grew serious. "I'm glad you stopped by. There's something I've been wanting to ask you."

"What?"

"Why did you run out on Emily the other night?"

Uh, oh. Should've known he'd bring that up. "It had nothing to do with her. Did she tell you what we were talking about?"

"Yes, and she was trying to sympathize with you." Gene's sharp voice irritated me. "She was wondering if she did or said anything wrong."

"No, she didn't. It was me. I thought about Granddad and the robbery, and I got upset. I had to get away."

"Will you please keep in mind that Emily's try-ing to get to know the family? She wants to fit in, so a little help would be appreciated. You know we're getting married in four months."

The lecture can stop any time. I walked to the door and yanked it open. "I promise I'll do better. Can you apologize for me?" Did I sound sincere?

"You can do that yourself at the next family dinner."

I closed the door on him.

Chapter 16

I stopped by Jim Thomas's office to see if he had any cheatin' spouse work, and he did have a case he wanted to hand off. "This gal's kind of a ditz-brain. Thinks her husband's cheating on her. Just call and tell her you're handling the case for me."

When I got back to the office, I dialed the number Thomas had given me. The woman, Shirley Chaney, said she'd stop by my office in the morning.

She came in soon after I opened up, and I could see why Jim had said she was ditz-brained. Dull brown hair fluttered out of the bun on the back of her head. The clothing tag on the back of her dress waved at me as I showed her to a seat, and her head jerked around as she looked over my office.

"This is awfully small. Are you sure you work with Mr. Thomas?"

"Yes." I smiled even though it hurt my face and my pride. "Sometimes Mr. Thomas gets busy and subcontracts with me. Now tell me why you think your husband may be stepping out on you."

"It's hard to talk about." I pushed a box of tissue toward her, just in case. "Steve's always been such a good husband, but lately he's been acting strangely."

"How so?"

"He's been going out three nights a week. There's always some excuse, but I notice it's the same three nights every week. He works in an office building with some very attractive single women. I'm afraid he's become attracted to one of them." She started crying.

I handed her a bottled water from the small refrigerator in my office and waited for her to get control of herself. "What three nights does he go out?"

"Monday, Wednesday, and Friday."

"Does he leave from the house every time?"

"Yes."

"Okay. That leaves me Wednesday and Friday to figure out what's going on. Hopefully it's nothing, but I'll get right on it for you."

She looked grateful as she signed the contract and gave me her address.

Wednesday night I parked a few doors down from the Chaney house. It seemed odd to me that

Mr. Chaney would leave at the same time on the same days every week. Usually guys that cheated were a little more inventive than that. Then I saw Steve Chaney.

The man was the embodiment of the word 'nerd'. He was about five feet eight, thin, balding, and wore glasses. If any of the attractive single women Mrs. Chaney mentioned were captivated by him, he should be forever grateful.

I had no trouble tailing him until we got to an intersection in the middle of town. Apparently there'd been an accident, and a patrolman was directing traffic. Mr. Chaney got the go-ahead, but I didn't. By the time I could drive across the street, I'd lost him. I hoped Friday would go better.

Work at the food bank kept me busy Thursday and Friday. Then I was back on the Chaney case. This time I had no trouble keeping Steve in sight. He pulled up at a dance studio and parked. I parked behind him, pulled out the tiny camera I'd brought along, took a picture, and returned the camera to my purse.

I gave him a few minutes inside, then I entered the studio. Everyone was busy choosing partners for a ballroom dance class. Chaney was standing off to the side when I walked up to him.

"Hi," I greeted him. "I'm new here. What exactly do we do?"

He smiled—a quick, shy smile. "We're choosing partners for the mambo right now. Would you mind being my partner?"

"No. Sounds good to me."

We went on the dance floor. "Thanks," he gushed. "I usually have trouble finding a partner. I promise not to step on your toes."

The promise lasted about ten seconds.

"Sorry." His face turned red. "I don't know if I'll ever get the hang of this, but I've got to learn by the eighteenth."

"You have a deadline for a dance class? Why?" I started to steer him toward the wall so we could sit down, and he could get off my feet. Fortunately he was letting me lead.

"That's my wife's birthday, and I want to surprise her by taking her out dancing. She's always loved to dance, and I've never learned."

I felt a big grin spread over my face. I tried not to laugh. Claire Burton solves another big case. The cheating husband who turns out to be a Fred Astaire wannabe. After a few more turns around the dance floor, I looked at my watch and excused myself. No use putting my toes through any more torture. I called Mrs. Chaney and asked her to meet me at my office the next morning.

She came at the appointed time and sat down, rigid, in front of my desk. "Go ahead and get it over with. He's got a girl friend, doesn't he? Who is she?"

"Mrs. Chaney, relax." I smiled and told her about the dance class.

Her eyes misted. "That's so sweet!"

The tissue box went across the desk again.

"I should have known. He's always been so considerate and loving." Her face clouded. "But now the surprise is ruined." She gave me an angry stare. "You ruined my surprise!"

"Mrs. Chaney, I did nothing more than what you asked me to do. You should be happy that your husband is such a good man. Now if you'll please settle up, we can be finished with this."

She jumped out of her seat. "I'm not paying you for this! My husband wasn't cheating, and you ruined my birthday! There's no way I'm giving you a cent!" She huffed toward the door.

"Lady, I'm taking you to a bill collector!" I shouted as she slammed the door.

I left a message on weasel lawyer Flint's machine that he could jolly well help me collect on this bill. And he still hadn't paid me for the Talbott case.

Pounding the desk with my fists for a few minutes helped my mood. After beating up my desk, I looked at the calendar and smiled. The day was getting better. Clint Seabold should be back in town. I was so looking forward to talking with him. In preparation for our chat, I decided it would be a good idea to take my pals Mr. Smith and Mr. Wesson along. Clint looked like the kind of guy who could get ugly if he got cornered.

I drove to Clint's business—Highland Carving. Several medium-sized totem poles and other carved figures stood outside the shop. Inside, display cabinets held various carving knives and other tools. Different sizes and varieties of wood also sat on shelves ready for sale. As I entered, he looked up from a receipt book and gave me a hard gray stare.

"Hi, Clint. How was the trade show?"

He looked surprised. Good. Betty hadn't told him about our little chat.

"It was fine. How did you know?"

"Betty stopped by the office. Said you'd be out of town for about a week."

He came out from behind the counter. "I don't imagine Betty's visit was free."

"What do you mean?"

"This investigation is costing us an arm and a leg. I've already talked to Betty about it. The way things are going, pretty soon we'll have to mortgage our home."

"You may not believe this, but I do understand. I was at your house. I know how you live. Trust me. I'm trying to keep the tab down."

"Trust you!" He moved closer, squaring off against me. "You wear that fancy pager all the time, and God knows what other gadgets you've got you're charging us for. There's no way I believe you're not milking us dry."

"Pager? Oh, you mean this?" I pointed to my pump.

He nodded.

"This isn't a pager. It's an insulin pump." I then had to go through the same spiel I gave Harold Carpenter about the pump and my condition.

Clint eased up a little. "I'm sorry. It's just that this investigation has re-opened a can of worms I wish would stay closed. Betty can't think of anything else but finding Cindy's killer. I thought we were past that."

"How can you ever get past a child's death—especially a death like Cindy's?"

He shrugged. "I guess you can't."

"When I was at the house, you started to tell me about Cindy before Betty brought the coffee in. What did you think of your stepdaughter?"

He bit his lip and thought for a moment. "I think I started to tell you what a handful she was. She was a wild kid—running with the wrong crowd, maybe into drugs."

"It was my understanding that she was fine when you and Betty were first married. Betty said she didn't go crazy until later on."

Clint turned away from me and started straightening shelves. "Her memories and mine are different."

"Betty said Cindy was on the streets for a while. Did you see her at all during that period?"

"No. We lost touch with her like Betty said. It wasn't 'til she straightened out that I saw her a few times."

I moved closer to him. "Don't jerk my chain. I know about your little shopping trip to West Indalia."

He wouldn't look at me. "What do you mean?"

"I know that Cindy saw you trying to pick up a hooker."

He whirled around, and I saw that deer-in-the-headlights look I always love seeing when I interrogate a suspect.

"It's not what you think. I can explain."

I expected him to get down on his knees and beg for mercy any second.

Rats! Somebody came in the store.

I wasn't going to let him off the hook. I whispered in his ear, "You'd feel a lot better if you'd just tell me the truth."

He shook me off. "I can't right now." He started toward the customer.

"When?" He could see I wasn't giving up.

"I'll meet you at that place—Dewey's—where we met before. I'll be there at noon, I promise." He put on a smile for the shopper.

I couldn't force him to talk to me, so I left. The odds were slim to none that he'd show up, but I had no other choice than to trust him.

My regular table was in use when I got to the restaurant, so I slid into a booth.

Dewey came over with the menu.

"Hey, Dewey. How dare you let anyone else sit at my table?"

"Pay me a hundred dollars, and it's yours forever."

"If I pay you a hundred dollars, I'll take the table with me when I leave. By the way, I think somebody may join me, so you might as well bring another menu."

"Is it Don?"

"No, it isn't Don, Mr. Nosy. It's business." I ordered then looked at my watch every five minutes until twelve thirty. Clint wasn't coming.

I called the store on the off chance he was running late. Betty answered.

"You mean you missed him? He was here this morning. He got a call that his aunt was very ill and in the hospital. He rushed off to be with her."

Sure he did.

I paid the tab and went back to Highland Carving. Betty was busy putting away a shipment of supplies when I came in. I asked her for a list of Clint's relatives and their contact information. I promised her I'd try not to bother him. "I only need to know which store he went to for those drinks. Shouldn't take more than five seconds to get an answer."

She pointed to a name on the list. " He said he might be going back and forth between the hospital and his aunt's house. He told me to call this number if I needed to reach him."

Time to call in the cavalry. Outside in the car, I phoned Don and left a message. Clint's abrupt disappearance made him the prime suspect in Cindy's murder. The police needed to know what was going on.

Don called my cell phone later. I filled him in on the details of what Little Billy had told me, and Clint's subsequent disappearance. "Your hunch about Seabold was right."

"Sounds like it. Great work, Claire. I'll put out an APB, and we'll see if we can scoop him up."

"Okay if I check around the relatives' houses to see if he shows up?"

"That might not be a good idea. We want this collar to stand up in court."

"I promise—if I see him, I'll call you immediately."

"Well, okay. It's always good to have as many eyes as possible on the street."

As I drove back to my apartment, I realized my schedule would be rough until Clint was caught. I'd spend some time at the food bank during the day, get some sleep, then stake out Clint's relative's house at night. I didn't think he'd be dumb enough to show up at the contact number house. But you never know.

Chapter 17

Next morning I bolused my insulin as usual while fixing breakfast. I was halfway through my oatmeal when the phone rang.

"Hi. It's Irene. Could you come down right away? My early morning volunteer hasn't shown up, and the delivery truck's here."

I wiped my mouth with a napkin. "Sure, I'll be right there."

"Thanks. You're a lifesaver!"

When I arrived, Irene was working with her usual precision—loading the dolly, dumping the cartons for Harold to put up, and rolling the dolly back to the truck. I pitched in and, gradually, the truck emptied.

As I was rolling one load toward Harold, he gestured. "Put it here, Claire. It'll be easier for me to put on the shelves."

"Yes sir, mon capitan. Anything you say." I saluted. *What a jerk. Can't he see how hard I'm working?* I started back toward the truck. "Irene, can you please move? I'm trying to get through."

Both Irene and Harold stopped working and stared at me.

I glared back. "What's your problem?"

"We'd like to ask you that question," said Harold. "You're biting our heads off."

"I am?" I stopped and noticed I felt shaky. Uh oh. Shaky and irritable. Not good. I went to my purse, retrieved my meter, and checked my sugar. Sixty-five. Time to treat. "I'm sorry." I reached in my purse for some glucose tablets. "My sugar's running low. Makes me crabby." I chewed the tablets. "I'll be better in a few minutes." I went to the break area and sat down.

Harold came over. "I thought the pump was supposed to level out your blood sugar."

He made me think. What had gone wrong? Ah, yes. "I know what happened. I should have finished my breakfast before I came over. I didn't eat enough to cover the insulin."

"I'm so sorry, Claire." Irene patted my shoulder. "If I'd known there'd be a problem, I wouldn't have called."

"No, no." I stood and gave her a hug. "It was my own fault. I should know better by now." I headed toward the door. "I think I'll take a break, so I don't have any more difficulties."

"Sure," Harold said. "Take your time."

I headed across the street to the diner.

"Hey, Claire." Little Billy sidled out of the alley.

"Why is it you always know when it's the wrong time to talk to me?"

"But I got somethin' important to tell you about C. K. Might be worth a Grant."

"You're too late, Billy. I'll buy you a meal, but that's it."

"That's better than nothin'."

We ordered up, then he asked me, "Why'd you say it was too late."

"Because it looks like your 'chunky dude' murdered C. K."

"How 'bout that? So I helped you, huh?"

"Yeah, you did." We high-fived.

"Guess what I had to tell you isn't important then."

"Go ahead. You never know."

"I saw the dude that runs the food bank drag somethin' heavy out the back one night."

"So what? Maybe he was taking out the trash."

"Don't think so. He put whatever it was in his car."

I shrugged. "Could have been anything."

"Yeah, you're right." We finished eating, and I went back to the food bank for a few more hours.

After helping out, I headed home for a nap before night patrol.

The phone was ringing as I entered my apartment. "Hello."

"Hi, Claire. It's Gene. You know that report you gave me to look at?"

"Yeah."

"Something doesn't make sense. I was wondering if you could get me all the balance sheets for the past year? I'd like to do some comparisons."

"Sure. Okay if I mail them? I'm kind of busy now right now."

"That'll be fine."

I hung the phone up and made a note to myself to ask Irene for the reports. The cop in me wondered if either Harold or Irene was ripping off the food bank. No. They were too dedicated to the people in West Indalia. I hit the sack.

The pattern was the same for the next week or so. I worked at the food bank during the day, took a nap, then pulled an all-nighter at one of Clint's relatives' houses. I took my gun along for company on the stakeouts. Never know who might decide to jump in your car at two o'clock in the morning.

One particular evening, I chose the contact number house as my target. About one o'clock, I saw some movement. A stocky man crept up on the porch and took out a key.

I'll be. Clint is dumb enough to come to this house. I put in a call to Don. No answer, of course, so I called the desk and told them the story. They said they'd contact him. Meanwhile I could see Clint was having trouble with the lock. I didn't want him to get away. I eased out of the car and sneaked up behind him.

"You stood me up for lunch, Clint. That wasn't polite."

He jumped and dropped the key. The porch light came on. A woman opened the door. "Clint, I heard noises out here."

Clint pushed past her. I could see her open-mouthed stare as I followed him inside. "What's going on?" she asked. "Clint…?" He tried to run out the back.

I drew my gun. "Stop right there." He saw the pistol and stopped.

"Clint, what is going on?" The woman's voice shook.

"Ma'am, it's all right." I spoke softly, trying to calm her. "Just go on upstairs and everything will be fine."

She headed up the stairs. As soon as she was out of sight, she yelled, "I'm calling the police."

"I already have, ma'am," I shouted back. "They should be here any minute."

I motioned toward a chair with my gun. "Why don't you have a seat? I'd like to continue the conversation we started in your shop."

Clint wilted into the chair. I holstered my gun. "You ran away, Clint. That looks bad. I think you'd better start talking."

Tears formed in Clint's eyes. "I told you, it's not what you think. I didn't hurt Cindy." He cried for a bit, then wiped his nose on his sleeve. "Well, maybe I did hurt her."

"What's that mean? Either you did or you didn't."

Clint rocked back and forth in his chair. "This is so hard. I don't know if I can…" He clenched his fists and closed his eyes tight.

I took a step toward him. "Clint, talk to me! Tell me what you did to Cindy!"

He started crying again and began shaking—disintegrating right in front of me. "I can't keep this inside any more. It's eating me alive." He took a long, shaking breath.

"Here's what happened." He wiped his eyes with his hands. "Like Betty said, everything was great for about the first six months of our marriage. We were a happy family. Then one day I walked in on Cindy when she was getting out of the shower. I didn't realize she was in the bathroom. She was standing there naked, and she was beautiful." He shuddered. "I only saw her for a few seconds before she covered herself and I closed the door, but it was enough. I couldn't get the sight of her body out of my mind."

I knew what he was going to say next, and I didn't want to hear it. Rage started to build within me.

He reached in his pocket for a handkerchief. "Finally, I cracked. I went to her room one night, and I…I…."

"You what?" I stood over him, every muscle tensed.

"I clamped one hand over her mouth and I—I forced myself on her." He began crying again.

I wanted nothing more than to jam my fist down his throat clear up to the elbow. It took all the control I had to restrain myself. After a few minutes, I settled down enough to speak. "That's when she started getting wild, wasn't it?"

He nodded, still crying.

I grabbed his shirt collar. "Look at me!"

He stared up, afraid.

"How many times did it happen?"

"Just once, I swear."

"I'll bet." I yanked on his shirt, pulling him closer to me.

"It's the truth!"

I eased up a bit. "Did Betty know what happened?"

"No. I warned Cindy if she told Betty about it, I'd say it was a lie. I'd say Cindy was trying to break up our marriage."

I tightened my grip again. *Unbelievable.* "What about your little journey down to West Indalia?"

"Betty was upset about Cindy and what she was doing. She didn't have any energy left for us and our relationship. I'd gone for a few months without any intimacy and got the urge."

I shook my head. "You're a real gem, Clint."

"Listen. You've got to hear me out," he pleaded. "I knew what I was doing was wrong. And when I saw Cindy's face, I knew I had to get help. I started seeing a doctor."

"Please. You expect me to buy that?"

"It's the truth."

"What happened at the boat landing? I know you were gone for about an hour."

"I got some of the same urges, so I went to my doctor right away."

"Does Betty know about the therapist?"

He shook his head.

I heard Don's voice at the door. "Police."

"Come on in, Don. The dirtbag's right here."

Don came in, arrested Clint and Mirandized him. He led Clint out in handcuffs. After Don put him in the car, I filled him in on what Clint had told me.

"Sounds open and shut. He'll probably admit to the murder in a few hours. Good job, Claire. I'll let you know how it goes."

They drove off. Motive, means, opportunity—it had all come together. Clint obviously didn't want Cindy spilling the beans to Betty. And one of those pieces of wood in his shop would make a dandy weapon to clobber someone with. I was sure it wouldn't take Don long to get the rest of the story out of Clint.

I pulled Cindy's picture from my purse and stood under the streetlight looking at her face—looking at the promise of a life that would never be. At least I was able to do one thing for her.

We got him, Cindy.

CHAPTER 18

The next morning, I couldn't get to my office fast enough. When Clint confessed and word got around that I'd solved the case, I knew my phone would be ringing off the hook. Sure enough, when I sat down at my desk, I saw the number two flashing on the answering machine. Business coming in already. As I grabbed a pencil to take down the messages, the phone rang. I picked up the receiver and gave my best professional greeting.

A familiar voice yelled in my ear. "Claire, this is Don. What were you thinking?"

"What do you mean?"

"Did you pull a gun on Seabold last night?"

"Yeah. He was trying to make a run for it." Why was Don so mad? "I wanted to keep him there until you arrived."

"And you questioned him?"

"Yes. What about it?"

"Seabold lawyered up when we got to the precinct. As soon as the attorney found out you'd pulled a gun on his client, he said whatever Seabold admitted to during that interview was coerced. Said Seabold was afraid of you and would have told you anything."

"You know what he told me was true." Lawyers!

"I know, but he said if we had you on the witness list, he'd make a motion to declare your testimony inadmissible."

I couldn't speak for a moment. What had I done?

"Claire? Are you still there?"

"Yes, I'm still here." I could hardly get the words out.

"Why couldn't you just sit in the car and observe him or follow him if necessary 'til I got there?"

"I guess it was a case of old reflexes coming into play. I wasn't thinking."

"You can say that again!" Don's words hammered at my heart. "The assistant D. A. doesn't think he can build a case without Seabold's admission that he sexually abused his stepdaughter."

"I don't know what to say," I mumbled.

"Well, congratulations, Claire. The guy who murdered Cindy Kagel is going to walk out of here a free

man, and there's nothing anyone can do about it."
The slammed-down phone made me jump.

I sat at my desk, numb. There was no way to fix
this mess—no way to make it right. I'd blown the
biggest case I'd probably ever investigate. It was over.
What could I do now? I sat for a few minutes trying
to shake off my anger at myself for being so stupid.
Finally I decided to see what the phone messages
were.

The first one was from Betty Seabold. After cuss-
ing me out for having her husband arrested, she fired
me. The second was from Gene. He wanted to talk
about the food bank's books at our family dinner
tonight.

I had nothing else to do. I decided to put Cindy's
file in order, then store it away. I never wanted to see
it again.

I took her picture from my purse. Her smiling,
innocent face, full of possibilities, looked back at me.
Once she'd been a bright girl with a future and a loving
boyfriend—the world waiting for her to explore it.
She'd ended up a corpse floating in four feet of water.
Now she wouldn't even get justice.

Sobs shook my body. I put my hands to my eyes
and felt the tears soaking my palms. I'd have to live
for the rest of my life with the knowledge that Cindy's
killer was walking free. And it was all my fault.

The crying stopped after awhile. I put Mahler's Tenth Symphony in the CD player—a piece of music unfinished like Cindy's life and this case. As I started to the file cabinet with Cindy's folder, a sheet of paper floated to the ground. It was the paper the Seabolds had found in Cindy's apartment. A loose end.

I took the paper back to the desk and studied it. Maybe unraveling this note Cindy left would make me feel better. *Let's see. The initials HC.* I began to jot things down.

Might stand for Highland Carving, Helen Colson, or Harold Carpenter. The next set—CRF. The only thing I could come up with was Computer Reasoning Factor. Then there was FBI. I thought for a while. Could be Firm Bodies, Inc., First Bank of Indalia, or Food Bank for Indigents. It could also stand for our friends, the fibbies, despite what Don had said. Nothing fit together. What were you trying to tell us, Cindy? Clicking my pencil on my teeth, I studied the sheet for some time, then gave up. *This is getting you nowhere, Claire.*

I went home, put on Mozart's Requiem, and sat curled up on the couch with a blanket tucked around me. After a while the music stopped, and I was conscious of the clock ticking in my bedroom. I looked at my watch. Six o'clock. Better get ready to go to the folks' for dinner. I dreaded telling them I was off the case, but they'd find out sooner or later. I should be the one to inform them.

As I drove over, I thought about the office. I certainly wasn't going to ask Betty Seabold for the money she owed me, and I couldn't keep going much longer on the money I had. I'd have to get a job. It was time to think about shutting down the business. Hopefully the landlord and I could work something out regarding the lease.

They were all in the living room when I walked in. Mom jumped up to embrace me. "Claire, you're early!" When she saw my face, she was startled. "Honey, what's the matter? Your eyes are all red. Have you been crying?"

I dissolved in her arms. Everyone gathered around trying to comfort me. I finally shook them off and made it to the couch.

Mom started fussing over me. "Are you sick?"

Dad handed me a box of tissues, and I got myself under control. "I'm off the Kagel case." My voice was flat.

"What?" asked Gene. "How'd that happen?"

I looked at my family gathered around me, love and concern on their faces, and I felt renewed shame. "I'd rather not talk about it now."

"Can we help in any way?" Dad's arm went around my shoulders.

I shook my head. "I'm going to have to close the office."

Emily took my hand. "What will you do?"

"I don't know. I'll figure something out."

We went to the table and ate in silence for a while. After dinner, Gene shifted in his chair. "Claire, is it all right if I ask you about something? I don't want to upset you tonight."

I welcomed the conversation. "Sure, Gene. Go ahead."

"You know I've been looking at the food bank's books. They don't add up, and I'm not talking about math here."

"What's wrong?"

"I checked the city budget. There's a contingency fund for the food bank, and there is enough money for another salaried position."

"You're kidding! Harold's always saying how broke the bank is. He told Irene they couldn't afford to replace Cindy."

"Sometimes contingency fund means slush fund. I'd like to look at some bank statements to see where the money's going."

"I'll see, Gene. I don't feel like playing detective right now." I went outside for some fresh air. After a few minutes, Emily was at my side.

"I should apologize for leaving you at the restaurant the other night." I couldn't look at her.

"It's okay." She put her arm on my shoulder. "I understand. You talked to me about a painful memory."

I pulled away.

She gave short laugh. "You remind me of a cat I once had. He was half-wild and didn't like to be touched. He tried to pretend he didn't care if I was around or not. But when I'd come home, he'd purr like crazy."

"What's your point?"

"Just remember that your family loves you. It's okay to reach out to them when you need them."

I closed my eyes to prevent the tears from falling again. "You're right, Emily." My voice was raspy. "Gene's lucky to have you." I hugged her.

Finally the evening was over. As I drove home, I thought about what Gene had said regarding the food bank books. Could Harold or Irene be ripping the city off? And why would they?

More importantly, did I want to dig into the bank finances? I'd already made a mess of the Kagel case. Maybe it was time to get out of the crime fighting business.

I spent the night curled up on the couch under the blanket again.

CHAPTER 19

The sunlight woke me. I'd slept fitfully. Don's voice kept echoing in my dreams, reminding me of how I'd botched everything. I winced as I climbed off the couch. My muscles ached from sleeping on the soft cushions. What a difference waking up this morning. I thought about how excited I was to get to work yesterday. I was going to be the biggest P. I. in the area. Now I would be lucky to last out the month in my office.

I did the usual morning things and wondered what I was going to do with my day. I didn't want to go to the office. My back didn't want me to lie on the couch any more. I decided to head to the food bank. Not much there I could screw up. I only hoped Irene would be on time today.

The door was still locked when I arrived. I groaned. Irene was a dear soul, but punctuality wasn't one of her virtues. I paced back and forth in front of the building. She finally drove up and jumped out of the car.

"I'm sorry. Running late again. Teenagers! They can't find anything." She unlocked the door, then looked at my face.

"What happened to you? Looks like you haven't slept in a week."

"Yesterday wasn't one of my better days. Let's just leave it at that."

"Okay. Do you feel like bagging?"

"Sure, let's get to it."

We worked in silence. I didn't feel like talking, and Irene sensed it. As we loaded the canned goods, my old instincts started kicking in. Was something funny going on with the food bank finances? Harold would be the most likely suspect if money were missing, although Irene might want money more than another employee to help her.

What the heck. I'll be out of this profession shortly. Might as well have a last hurrah and investigate the great Food Bank for Indigents Embezzlement Caper.

"May I make a suggestion, Irene?"

"Sure, go ahead."

"Since your kids make you run late sometimes, how about giving me a key? I'll be working here a couple of days a week for a while. I can help you out by opening the place."

She smiled. "That's a great idea. I'll go get Cindy's key for you."

The mention of Cindy's name hurt. Here I was on some half-baked wild goose chase, and I'd let Cindy down so badly. Irene handed me the key, and I stared at it remembering that a nice kid who met a horrible death had once held it.

"Anything wrong?"

"No. I'm fine." I turned from her and put the key in my purse.

When the food shipment arrived, Harold came down from his office and helped us unload. We worked as a team to unload the truck, our movements almost choreographed because we'd done the same chore together so many times. After we finished, Harold went back to his office.

I went to the break area for some coffee. "Does Harold ever relax?" I asked Irene. "I never see him take time off. He's either down here unloading, or talking to the kids, or in his office doing paperwork."

Irene joined me. "That's Harold. He's working hard now to get a kids' fund established."

"Really? What would the fund be for?"

"He's always been interested in the kids and their futures. He'd like to set up a place where they could go after school. He's envisioned a center where the kids could participate in supervised sports and games. He even wants to include special tutoring for those who need it."

"Wow! The works, huh?"

"Yes. That's why he was so upset when the budget was cut. He doesn't have any hope that the city would fund such a project."

So she doesn't know about the contingency fund or the money budgeted for another employee. "I wouldn't count Harold out. Maybe he can pull a rabbit out of his hat, yet."

"He might. If there's a way to do it, Harold will find it," she agreed. She looked at her watch. "Is it okay if I go to lunch first? I'm really hungry today."

"Sure." *Please go to lunch. I want a look at those files upstairs.*

She left, and I went upstairs to Harold's office. "Irene asked me to dig out some notes while she was gone. She wants to make sure she thanked everyone for their donations."

Harold looked up from a folder. "Go right ahead. Everything's in those file cabinets."

I wanted to see where the bank statements were kept. Since Irene didn't seem to know about the extra funding, I suspected something funny might be going on. I needed Gene's expert help in determining how the money was flowing in and out. The files were in impeccable order. It was easy for me to find what I needed after looking through a few drawers. I removed some papers to make it look good. "I think this is what she's looking for. You know, these files are in amazing order. You must be a neat freak."

Harold smiled.

"How did you find time to organize them?"

"I didn't. Cindy Kagel, that poor girl who drowned, was an employee here right before her death. She worked out the filing system."

"Ah, yes. I remember Irene telling me about her. She must have been a good worker."

"She was for a while, then she started not showing up on time. Had trouble doing the books. She became unreliable."

"Why did she, do you think?"

"I think she went back on drugs. I was about ready to fire her when she died."

I went downstairs and poured another cup of coffee. Something didn't make sense. Harold told me Cindy was coming unraveled. Everyone else had told me Cindy had straightened up. Harold also hadn't used the word 'murder' when he spoke of her. *Get off it, Claire! You know who killed Cindy. You're trying to dream up suspects to make yourself feel better.* I tucked the papers I'd taken from the files in my purse. I'd return them later when I made another visit to the office.

Irene came back from lunch, and we began working again. "I was talking to Harold while you were gone. He told me something interesting about Cindy Kagel."

"What?"

"He said he couldn't depend on her any more. He was getting ready to fire her."

Irene stopped arranging food on the shelves and turned, eyes wide with surprise. "What! Cindy? No way! You could set your watch by her. She always did a good job, too."

"I'm just telling you what he said. Maybe, since he was her supervisor, he saw things you didn't."

"Maybe, but I still don't believe it."

"Okay if I go home now? I'm kind of tired."

Irene agreed, and I left. Yesterday's emotions and last night's lack of sleep had caught up with me.

When I got home, I noticed there was a message on the answering machine from some reporter wanting to interview me. I hit the delete button, put on some quiet Sibelius selections, and tried to turn off my mind.

The phone woke me up next morning. At least I'd slept through the night. Dad was on the other end. "Did I wake you?"

"Yes, but that's okay."

"I think you'd better look at the paper, honey. There's something about you in it."

"About me? What is it?"

"It concerns that Kagel case you were working on. If you need to talk after you read it, give me a call. The family's behind you one hundred percent."

It must really be bad. Maybe I should have called that reporter back. I got dressed and fortified myself with a cup of tea before I picked up a paper.

Apparently the reporter had been at the station when Clint was brought in. Since he recognized the name Seabold from Cindy's murder case, he started nosing around. Clint's lawyer was only too happy to be interviewed. He said he was thankful that the police recognized his client had been terrorized. The reporter also interviewed Clint's relative. She said she feared for her life that night. I was 'unavailable for comment'. The article made me sound like a vigilante charging into a house with gun drawn, threatening innocent citizens.

I threw the paper across the room and said a few choice words about reporters. I knew I'd have to explain what happened to my family, but decided I needed breakfast among friends at Dewey's first.

Dewey saw me when I came in. "You okay, Claire?" he asked as he showed me to my table. *Great. Everybody's probably read the story.*

I studied the menu for a bit, then looked around the room. A few acquaintances met my gaze and smiled. Most looked away or scowled at me. Cathy was working the other side of the restaurant. I could tell if I was the last customer in the world, she still wouldn't have waited on me. *I don't need this.* Dewey came toward me with an order pad, but I was already on my feet.

"I'm not hungry today, Dewey. Maybe next time." He looked sad as I passed him. At least I had one friend.

Of course, my sugar was way too high when I checked it. Nothing like stress to move those numbers right up there. I dumped some cereal and milk in a bowl, covered the elevated sugar and the meal with an insulin bolus, and started eating.

The thought kept whirling in my mind. *What are you going to do now?* I absentmindedly stirred the cereal as I contemplated my options. There weren't many. All I'd ever wanted to do was be in law enforcement. I wasn't trained for anything else. Normally I'd apply for a security guard position, but I doubted anyone would hire me for that job right now. I also knew I couldn't get the desk job I'd been offered at the station.

An idea popped into my head. Maybe I could get a job related to the things I'd learned at the food bank. I could talk to Irene and Harold about the possibility the next time I saw them. I felt better. I had a plan. There was one hurtful chore I had to do first, though. Pack up my office.

CHAPTER 20

I spoke to the landlord the next day about breaking the lease. He was very accommodating. I figured he was afraid I'd shoot up the place if he crossed me.

Armed with some boxes, I took the next few days to pack everything and clean the office. It was quiet with no CD player hooked up and the phone disconnected. I'd gotten some ugly gloating messages from people I'd arrested in the past, so I no longer wanted to listen to the answering machine.

Finally everything was ready to be carried to the car. I was leaving the furniture until Dad and Gene could help me load it up. I took out what few boxes I had and put them in the car. It was pathetic. All the work I'd put into that office could be held in the trunk of a Saturn. I went back and, with tears in my eyes, pulled the Claire Burton, Private Investigator placard out of its holder by the door. It was over.

The next day I went to the food bank ready to pepper Irene with questions about a possible job. When I entered, Harold and Irene were talking. They stopped speaking and looked at me, stone-faced. *Oh boy, they've seen the article.*

Harold approached, hands on hips. "Do you enjoy making us look like fools, Claire?"

"What do you mean?"

"Don't act innocent with us. We saw the article in the paper. You knew about Cindy Kagel before you ever started working here. You played us, Claire."

Irene came up to join him. "I feel betrayed. Why didn't you tell me who you were? I would have answered your questions."

For the first time, I felt guilty about conducting an investigation. I knew Irene was right. She would have told me anything I wanted to know. I was also panicky. This might be my last chance to train for another job. I'd have to smooth things over somehow.

"I don't blame you both for being mad at me." I motioned toward the break area. "Can we sit down and talk about it?"

They reluctantly followed me to the chairs and sat like judges waiting for me to explain myself.

"The reason I didn't tell you who I was is because I'm used to folks not telling me the truth when I ask questions. When I was a cop, there weren't very many people who ran up to me and said, 'Please arrest me. I did it'." Irene and Harold smiled.

"You must believe me, though, when I tell you that I genuinely enjoy volunteering down here." I was practically on my knees. "I didn't have to come to West Indalia that often to find out what I needed to know about Cindy, but I discovered I truly enjoy working with you. If you'll allow me, I'd like to continue helping out until I can find a job."

Harold and Irene looked at each other. "What do you think, Harold?

"I personally have my doubts," Harold groused. "I can't help wondering what else she's lied to us about."

"But what would she have to gain by working here? It's not like we have anything to hide."

Harold gave Irene a look.

"Come on, Harold. My volunteer didn't show up today."

"Oh, all right. We'll see how it goes."

Irene rose and headed toward the work area. "What are you waiting for, Claire? Get bagging."

I hugged them both. "Thanks for under-standing."

Irene and I gabbed about her kids and my situation and worked the morning away. When I was at lunch, my cell phone rang. I dug it out of my purse.

"Hi, Claire," said Gene. "I've been trying to get hold of you for several days. What's with your office phone?"

I explained to him what had happened and informed him he was going to be moving furniture soon.

"Goody, I can hardly wait." He laughed then became serious. "I'm truly sorry about everything. Is there anything Emily and I can do?"

"Just be there. That's enough." *Thanks, big brother.* "By the way, why did you call?"

"I was wondering when you'd get those bank statements to me."

The statements! I'd forgotten about them. "It'll take me a few more days, but I'll round them up for you." As I hung up, I realized I had a new mission. I now wanted to prove my friends Harold and Irene innocent of any wrongdoing.

CHAPTER 21

I decided it would be wise to play it cool for a while. Harold and Irene were outwardly friendly, but still a bit suspicious of me. I couldn't blame them. They felt betrayed. Best not to rock the boat and look through files right now. Besides I had other concerns. My money was dwindling fast. Lawyer Flint had finally paid up, and he was my last source of income.

After we'd finished handing out food one day, I spoke to Irene. "Irene, I'm in a bind right now. I have no money coming in. Do you know of any other charitable organizations in town that have paid employees?"

"Each group has a director who's salaried. I don't know what other paid workers they might have, since everybody's different. I can give you a list with some names. You could check and see what the possibilities are."

"Thanks. I'd appreciate it."

She went to the office and gave me a directory of the charities in town. "Things getting tight for you?"

"Yeah. I'm about to be cancelled by my health insurance, and it's not cheap to wear an insulin pump."

She made a face. "No insurance. That's not good. Do you have any other options?"

"I could go back on the shots, but I'd rather not. The pump is so much more convenient for my lifestyle."

"Then I hope you can stay on it." We started back to the work area "I'm curious, Claire. Why are you looking for jobs with charities?"

"I've been considering my options. I was trained to go after the bad guys. It's what I know, but I also know nobody will hire me for police work now. Not after that blasted newspaper article came out. I was thinking since I had some experience working here and I really enjoy it, maybe someone would hire me."

"It's possible, but I can tell you most of the groups here have only one or two paid staffers. You might need to volunteer with them to work your way in."

"Guess I'll have to check everything out." I stuffed the list in my purse. "Thanks for your help." We went back to work.

One day Harold came down from his office dressed in suit and tie. "Pretty spiffy, Carpenter," I said. "What's the occasion?"

"I'm giving a presentation to a local service club. I've got to look good for that."

Irene brushed some lint from his shoulder. "Harold's trying to raise money for his children's project. He's hoping the service groups here will take the project on as a fundraising activity."

"Good luck, then."

"Thanks." He laughed as he started toward the door. "I figure I can't lose. At least I'll get a free lunch."

Irene grabbed her purse. "Think I'll go to lunch, too. Is that okay with you?"

"Sure. I'll hold down the fort."

It was too good an opportunity to miss. I made sure both Irene and Harold were well out of sight before I went up to the office. I pulled a folder out of the file cabinet and made copies of the bank statements, then checked through the files to see if there was something else interesting I should be showing Gene. Nothing appeared odd or out of place. I replaced the folder and the papers I'd taken previously and tidied up.

I left when Irene returned. It was Tuesday, and I was going to see the folks. Gene would be there so I could give him the statements. I hoped he wouldn't be too embarrassed when he looked them over and realized he'd made a big mistake.

Everyone else was already there when I arrived at my folks' house. We talked for a while about what I was going to do next, and I appreciated their concern. It was like being wrapped in a warm fuzzy blanket. I handed Gene the bank statements, and we went in to eat.

The conversation turned to Gene and Emily's wedding. Emily and Mom took over with a vengeance. I honestly tried to keep up with them because I knew the wedding was important to the family, but I got lost after the discussion focused on bridesmaids' dresses and empire waistlines. My mind drifted to my job situation.

"Would that work for you, Claire?" Emily's voice interrupted my thoughts.

"What?" I realized all faces at the table were looking at me. I'd missed something. "I'm sorry. What did you say?"

Gene's face reddened. "For crying out loud, Claire! I'm sorry about your situation, but can't you for once pay attention to somebody beside yourself? Emily and I are getting married. We happen to think that's a rather important event. We're trying to include you, but you're staring off into space, ignoring everybody."

A tear rolled down my cheek. He was right. I squeezed Emily's hand. "Please forgive me. I really am excited about your wedding. It's just that I don't know that much about these kinds of things." I dabbed at the moisture on my face with my napkin. "Let's put it this way. You turned right at inverted pleats, and I took a left."

Emily smiled and squeezed back. "I understand. You have a lot on your mind right now."

"Now what did you want to know?" I asked, grateful for her patience.

"I was wondering if the gown would be a problem with your pump."

"I don't see why. Do you have a picture of the dress?" She pulled out a catalog and pointed to a drawing. It was a typical bridesmaid's dress—all fluffy and pouffy. Something I'd never wear again.

At this point though, I'd wear a dress made of sticks and leaves if it would make Gene and Emily happy.

"No problem at all." I smiled, hoping to calm Gene. "I can either wear the pump in my bra or on my thigh. Don't worry, I'll figure it out."

We spent the rest of the evening talking about guest lists, wedding cakes, and refreshments. I hung on every word.

Before I left, I warned my folks that I might need a loan.

CHAPTER 22

I started knocking on doors, looking for a job. Irene was right. The charitable organizations in town kept their expenses down by having only a few paid employees. I couldn't blame them, but it was frustrating watching the doors slam in my face. Maybe lunch with friends would help.

The cell phone rang as I pulled up to Dewey's. "Claire," Gene's voice crackled on the other end.

"I can't hear you, Gene. I'll call you back when I get to a regular phone." He probably wanted to apologize for all the fuss over the food bank's financials. I went to my apartment so I could talk with him privately and ease his embarrassment.

He answered the phone on the first ring. "Claire, is that you?"

"Yeah, what's up?" I waited for the 'I'm sorries' to begin.

"Can you come by my office sometime today?"

"Sure, right away. Why?"

"This thing is bigger than I thought. I need to go over what I found with you."

I sat on the couch, stunned. Gene kept a cool head around finances, yet he sounded agitated on the phone. What had he found? I hopped in the car and headed to Parkersburg.

When I entered his office, Gene pointed to some papers on his desk. "You've gotta see this." I moved my chair close to the desk so I could look at what he was talking about. He then launched into an explanation spoken entirely in accountantese. My head spun out after about five minutes.

"Hold it, Gene." I put up my hands to stop him from talking. "I don't understand what you're trying to tell me. Please give me the short version."

"Okay, here it is. There's money missing to the tune of the middle five figures."

I sat up straight. "What! Are you sure?"

He nodded. "I've gone over and over the books. I know what's coming in from the city budget. A lot of it isn't accounted for by the paperwork you gave me."

"Something's not right." I shuffled through the papers. "I can't believe either Harold or Irene would be ripping the city off."

"One plausible explanation is that there's another ledger somewhere. Did you check for other bookwork or statements from other banks?"

"I made a thorough search of the files. I couldn't find anything that would even hint at another account." I leaned back, chin cupped in my hand. *What's going on?* "Is there any other possibility?"

He thought for a moment. "Yes, there is. Maybe there's some program on the computer Harold and Irene use that we don't know about. The other account could be in that program. I don't understand why you wouldn't have bank statements for the account, though."

"Another program." Now it was my turn to think. I pictured Harold's messy office. Anything could be in there or on the computer. "I'll bet you're right, Gene. I don't know everything about the operation. There probably is another account I'm not aware of. There might be some files I don't know about, too." I was relieved. "I'm sure Harold and Irene have a logical explanation. I should have asked them about all this in the first place." I headed toward the door. "Thanks so much for all the time you put in on this."

"Wait a minute, Claire. Aren't your cop instincts kicking in? Maybe this discrepancy is innocent, but maybe it isn't. We might be looking at some pretty hefty embezzlement here."

I stopped, my hand still reaching for the door-knob. I turned slowly. Big brother had a point. "You're absolutely right. How would I uncover what's going on?"

"Obviously, you'll need to get into the computer. Would you like me to help you?"

"No. If you came over, that would raise suspicion. Just tell me what I'm looking for."

Gene showed me around his computer and gave me hints on where to look for programs. "The tough thing will be to log onto the computer in the first place. I'm sure Harold and Irene both have login names and passwords."

"They probably do. How do I get around that problem?"

"Most people aren't too sophisticated about their passwords. They'll use variations on their names, birth dates, or something else that's easy for them to recall. You must remember, though, that whatever's used will be case-sensitive."

"What do you mean by that?"

"Let's say you want your login name to be Claire, but you type it in using a small letter c. If anyone else comes along and tries to use your name, but types it in with a capital C, the computer won't like that."

"Good to know. I can't thank you enough, Gene. I'll definitely look into this."

I had a lot to think about as I drove back to Indalia. I'd let my guard down because I was desperate for friends after the newspaper article came out. I could never do that again. I hoped there was a legitimate account, but the amount of money Gene said was missing was too big to be ignored. Someone should investigate the matter. That someone would be me.

Chapter 23

I t felt good to be back in investigation mode if only for a short time. I knew I'd have to leave the food bank soon for some kind of paying job, even if it was flipping burgers. I only hoped I'd get the chance to do some computer searching before I had to quit.

Unfortunately, Harold was sticking pretty close to his office these days, taking breaks only to shoot some hoops with the kids at a park across the street. He even ate his meals at his desk. Ever since the newspaper article mentioning me had come out, he'd taken to spending more and more time upstairs.

After we finished handing out groceries one day, Irene fretted. "If Harold doesn't get out of that office soon, I'll never catch up on my work."

"Can't you ask him to give you some time on the computer, or better yet, get yourself another terminal?"

"I've already tried. He says he's got to spend a lot of time on his kids' fund. Naturally he also says we can't afford another computer."

"Those things are dirt cheap nowadays. I'll bet you could even get someone to donate one to you."

"I know," Irene agreed, "but tell that to Harold. He's got this kids' project stuck in his craw, and he can't seem to think about anything else." She started up the stairs. "You know what? I think I'll kick him out today. He needs my paperwork for his report to the board, and I'm tired of running behind."

"You go, girl." I laughed as she stomped up the stairs.

Harold came down a few minutes later, a pouty look on his face. "I'm going to lunch," he mumbled.

I darted up the stairs as soon as he left. "Hey, Irene," I called to her as she sat down at the terminal. "Mind if I look over your shoulder? Maybe some computer experience would help me get a job with one of the other groups."

"Sure, but please don't ask too many questions. I've got to get this stuff done in a hurry."

I promised her I'd try not to be a pest, then stood behind her and watched as she logged on. She used her first name with a capital I. I knew her password would be xed out, so I memorized which keys she hit.

She worked rapidly entering figures into different categories. "You're quick." I was impressed.

"Doesn't take me too long if I can get on this monster." She started explaining the account setup to me.

"How complicated is all this? I'm wondering if I'd have all different kinds of books to keep if I got a job with another charity?"

"I don't know about other groups, but we have just the one account here."

Only one account, huh. Gene was right to prod me to look into the food bank funds. I'd have to get into this computer somehow.

Later that week Harold drove up to the food bank in a van and began unloading boxes and suitcases. Irene looked as puzzled as I was.

"What gives?" I asked.

"You got me. Almost looks like he's moving in." She walked over to hold the door open for Harold as he continued to unload the van. "What's all this stuff, Harold?"

"I got permission from the city to live here. Since I'm saving money on rent, I'll be donating some of my salary to the children's project in return. That way we can get starting building sooner."

As Harold went toward the stairs, Irene followed him making the crazy sign with her forefinger to her temple.

We headed for the break area while Harold unpacked in his office.

Irene frowned as she stirred her coffee. "Harold's starting to scare me. He's become obsessed with this project."

"I've got to admit it seems nuts to me. Why would anyone in their right mind want to live here, even to get their dream going?"

"I don't think he's ever gotten over Ernie."

"Ernie? I never heard him mention that name. Who's Ernie?"

"Ernie was a boy who used to hang around here. He was about twelve years old—a darling kid. His mom was raising him right. Harold took a liking to him and spent a lot of time with him. He'd read to Ernie when he could, shoot hoops with him, that kind of thing." Irene poured another cup of coffee from the pot. "Then one day Ernie didn't show up.

Harold went looking for him and, unfortunately, found him."

"What do you mean, 'unfortunately'."

"Seems Ernie'd gone home to his apartment after school. He was alone because his mother was out trying to earn enough money to hold the family together. Somebody broke in while he was there by himself."

"That must have scared the kid to death."

"Wait. It gets worse. We found out later the creep had broken into the wrong apartment. He thought some people who'd ripped drugs off him lived there. He was out for revenge."

I winced. "I know from experience how ugly that situation can be. What happened to Ernie?"

She reached for a tissue and wiped the corner of her eye. "He got his brains blown out."

"Oh, no!" I put my arm around her shoulder.

"Harold was the one who found him. The sight of that poor boy changed him."

I guided her back to a chair. "I think seeing that would affect anyone."

She let out a ragged sigh. "He swore after that the kids here would have a safe place to go after school, no matter what it took."

No matter what it took. A man with a cause might do almost anything. I needed to get into that computer.

CHAPTER 24

I came to the food bank every day, hoping for an opportunity to get into the computer. Harold wasn't giving me that chance. He started sending Irene out for his meals, even making sure she brought him dinner before she left.

One night, as she was carrying in some Styrofoam food containers, I asked, "Do you think Harold's lost it? He hardly ever sticks his head out of his office any more."

"Frankly, he's scaring me, Claire. I've tried to think of ways to get him to relax, but I haven't come up with anything." She started toward the stairs with Harold's meal.

"Do you know if he likes any kind of entertainment? Maybe he'd like to see a movie or go to a concert."

She stopped and, smiling, looked back at me. "He loves classical music."

"Okay. I think there's a concert coming up at the college." I headed toward the door.

"Good luck," Irene called after me.

The college was indeed having a concert, so I bought a ticket I could ill afford, and brought it in to the bank.

Irene was ecstatic when I showed her the ticket. "This is great, Claire. Now maybe we can get Harold out of here so he can unwind. I'd like to see him in a better mood."

I'd like to see him out of the building. Harold was pecking away at the computer, as usual, when I entered his office. We exchanged how-are-yous then I got down to business. "I know you've been working hard, Harold. You haven't had much time for yourself lately, so I'd like to give you a chance to relax." I laid the ticket on his desk. "Since I heard you liked classical music, I got you a ticket to a concert this weekend."

He sat back in his chair; arms folded across his chest, anger hardening his face. "First it's Irene nagging me to get out of here, now it's you! I'll decide when it's time for me to take a break! Thanks, but no thanks." He threw the ticket at me.

I scooped it up and went back down to the work area. Irene was standing, wide-eyed, at the bottom of the stairs. "I could hear Harold shouting clear down here. What happened?"

"Apparently, Harold doesn't want to leave his office. I think he'd rather have a nervous breakdown." We spent the rest of the day in an uneasy truce, avoiding Harold's territory.

I decided to take a nap the next afternoon and stake out the food bank that night. Maybe Harold would slip out when he thought everyone was asleep. No such luck. After his office went dark, there was no further movement all night.

That morning, I went Little-Billy-hunting and finally found him on one of his favorite corners. His face lit up when he saw me.

"How you doin', Claire?"

He was no doubt fishing for another Grant. "I'm fine, Billy. Got a question for you."

"Sure. What is it?"

"You know Harold Carpenter, the guy that runs the food bank?"

He sneered. "You mean Mr. Fine Upstanding?"

"Why do you call him that?"

"Nobody's that good. He's got some angle."

"Maybe, but what I want to know is if you've ever seen him on the streets at night?"

Billy leaned his head, first to one side, then the other. "I don't rightly remember. I think better when I got somethin' in my stomach."

I pulled him into a burger joint. As he munched away on his sandwich, he said, "The dude used ta leave and go home at night. Now I don't see 'im on the streets at all."

"Can you keep an eye out for him the next few nights?" I reached in my purse and pulled out a twenty-dollar bill.

"A Jackson? That's all I'm gettin'? Grant was a lot better president than Jackson was."

"I'm on a budget, Billy. Take it or leave it." I started to put the money away.

"Okay. Better'n nothin', I guess." He snatched the bill from my hand.

I gave him my cell phone number, then slid out of the booth to get some shuteye.

The next day I got a call from a mental health clinic with a job offer. I'd be a full-time assistant. I told them I'd need a few days to close out my other activities then I'd be ready to start work.

Come on, Billy. Give me a call. I kept listening for the cell phone's ring, kept hoping I'd get one more chance to crack a case even if it was a small one. No word came from Billy. It was time to face facts. The great private investigator, Claire Burton, would have to leave crime fighting.

And after such a stellar career.

CHAPTER 25

I settled in at Indalia Community Counseling Center and began learning about my new job. I was surprised at how interesting the work was. Clients who came in appreciated the help they got from the Center, and I found that solving their problems helped me forget about my own circumstances. The old saying was certainly true. You could always find someone else who's worse off than you are.

There was an unexpected bonus to working at the Center. A young psychologist, Tom Brinley, also worked there. He was single, reasonably attractive, and kind. We began dating.

One night as we were coming home from a movie, he asked, "When am I going to meet your family?"

I grimaced. "Are you sure you want to be subjected to a Tuesday night dinner?"

"If I can counsel family members who are at war with each other, I can handle your folks."

"Good point." I gave his arm a quick squeeze. "I'll tell Mom to set an extra place this week." I didn't tell him that Mom had been pestering me to meet him ever since we'd started dating.

On Tuesday, we drove up to the house at the appointed time. I knew the folks would approve of Tom's conservative white shirt, tie, and gray trousers. His dark blue eyes, cocoa-colored hair, and lanky build wouldn't hurt anything either.

As we reached the house, I withdrew my hand from his to open the door. I didn't return my hand to his grasp. "You're not a touchy, feely kind of person, are you?" he asked.

"Guess not." We walked in the door. "Mom," I yelled down the hall, "we're here."

My parents came out from the kitchen and gave Tom a warm welcome. Gene and Emily were, of course, there for dinner, too. We settled in the living room and talked until Mom decided it was time to eat.

After dinner, I was helping clear the table when Gene motioned for me to step back into the living room.

"I'm dying to know, Sis, did you ever get into the food bank computer?"

"No, I never got the chance. Believe it or not, Harold actually started living in his office. I don't think he'd leave if the place caught fire."

"You're kidding! Don't you think that's strange?"

"Of course, I do! But since I'm a civilian, there's nothing I can do about it."

We sat down on the couch. "Did you try one of your detective tricks?"

"Yeah, I tried to coax him out with a concert ticket. He wouldn't go for it."

"Something's got to be up with those books," Gene said. "I'd love to get my hands on them."

"Watch out, Gene. You might catch the Claire Burton detective disease." We both laughed.

Tom came into the room. "What's so funny?"

"Just some brother-sister kidding around." I motioned for him to have a seat beside me. We spent the rest of the evening talking about Gene and Emily's wedding. The date was coming up fast, and preparations were proceeding at a frantic pace. I was given my assignments—to show up for my dress fitting and to attend Emily's shower. Tom and I left amidst handshakes and hugs from the rest of the family.

Tom opened the car door for me. "Your family's very friendly."

"Thank you. I'd say you passed their date-o-meter test with flying colors." I got in, and we drove to my apartment.

As I fumbled in my purse for the key, he took me in his arms and kissed me. "Can I come in?"

I withdrew from his embrace and unlocked the door. "Mind if I give you a rain check? I'm really bushed tonight."

He looked disappointed, but started down the hall. "Okay, see you tomorrow."

I made some tea and sat at the table sipping it, thinking about my life. I had a good job and had met a decent man. All in all, I'd settled into a quiet, comfortable existence. So then, why wasn't I happy? I dumped the rest of the tea in the sink and got ready for bed. The problem was my life was too quiet, too comfortable.

A few days later, Tom asked me to go to dinner at a newly opened restaurant. Indalia was still small enough that anything fresh and shiny attracted a horde, so the place was packed when we arrived. Fortunately we had a reservation. Even so, there was only one table left. As we sat down, I caught a glimpse of a man with very familiar broad shoulders and dark hair sitting a few tables over. It couldn't be!

I peeked out of the corner of my eye. It was. Don and his little Lori were also dining here. I hoped he hadn't seen me. Or maybe I did want him to see me—to see that I could get a date, too.

We studied our menus and gave our orders to the waiter. Tom started telling me about something that happened at work. His hand rested on the table, and I put mine over it while he was talking. He looked at our clasped hands and smiled as he gazed at my face.

He continued his story. I paid careful attention, drinking in every word. My laughter sparkled at the funny parts, and my eyes studied his at the serious parts. I also occasionally sneaked a look at Don's table. Was he seeing how wrapped up I was in Tom?

We finished eating and left. Don and Lori were still there, probably having dessert. *I hope she gains twenty pounds.*

After we got into Tom's car, he turned to me. "What's going on, Claire?"

"What do you mean?"

"All the time we've been dating, you've never paid as much attention to me as you did tonight. In fact, you've been pretty standoffish. Now, all of a sudden, everything I say fascinates you."

"I was interested in your story." I sounded lame, even to myself.

His tone grew sharper. "I also noticed you kept glancing at another couple sitting close to us. Did you by chance know the man who was at the table?"

Busted. Tom was too good a psychologist and way too observant. I nodded—my head down. "We used to be engaged." My voice was husky.

"I'm not into playing games, Claire. Have you been using me to get back at this other guy?"

"Oh, no, Tom!" I spoke rapidly. "I swear that wasn't my intention. But tonight when I saw him, something happened."

Tom started the car. "It's obvious to me that you aren't over him yet, so I think it's best that we keep our relationship professional for the time being."

I started crying.

He handed me a handkerchief.

I took off work the next day and went for a walk on the canal. Thoughts churned in my head about what might have been, and what my life had become. Once I'd been in perfect health; now I had diabetes. Once I'd had my dream job; now I worked at a job I'd settled for. Once I'd been engaged to a man I passionately loved; now I had no one.

The murky water lapped at the canal's edge—the same water that had held Cindy Kagel's body. I thought of Cindy, a bright girl who should have had a bright future. Then I thought of Betty Seabold, a grief-stricken mother who would never hold a grandchild in her arms. *Get over it, Claire. You still have a chance at a good life. Cindy's life never really got started, and Betty's life is ruined.*

Mentally, I kicked myself for a few minutes then sat down on a bench to read the newspaper. A familiar face pictured in the local news section caught my attention. Harold Carpenter was shown with his foot on a shovel breaking ground for a new children's center. In the article, he thanked everyone for their generous donations to the project and mentioned that more donations would be welcomed.

Betty Seabold had an ad in the classifieds saying she was no longer responsible for any debts other than her own. Maybe Clint had finally told her what happened with Cindy. I wanted to comfort Betty, but knew I'd only make matters worse. I took Cindy's picture out of my purse.

Sitting with her image in my hand, I took a good look at her and at my life. I made a decision. The best thing I could do now was to do the finest job possible at the Center and to be there for my family.

I picked up two stones and threw them in the canal. One to get rid of the angry Claire, and the other to get rid of the self-pitying Claire. I felt like a huge burden had been lifted from me. I felt free—able to do anything.

Watch out, world! Claire Burton's turning over a new leaf and coming on strong!

Chapter 26

With Gene's wedding only two weeks away, I was spending a lot of time at the folks' house. They knew I wasn't seeing Tom any more, so there was no discussion about him.

Emily was busy giving everyone chauffeuring schedules for picking up members of her family at the airport when the phone rang. Dad answered it, talked for a few minutes, then made a face and hung up.

"That's just great! In the middle of everything else we have going, my speaker dropped out for the club meeting. It's very short notice to arrange another program. Now what am I going to do?"

I didn't pay much attention to what Dad was saying. His problem was just another flap piled on top of all the other flaps the family had going. But suddenly a thought occurred to me.

"When do you have to have the speaker?" I asked.

"Day after tomorrow. Why?"

"I think I can get someone to fill in for your program."

Dad brightened. "Yeah? Who?"

"Remember Harold Carpenter, the guy I used to work with at the food bank?"

Dad nodded.

"He's always eager to talk about the new kids' center. I'll bet I can get him to speak to your group."

"Wasn't his picture in the paper recently?"

"Yes, at the groundbreaking. I'll warn you up front. He'll probably ask your group to do a fundraiser for the center."

"That's all right. We're used to that."

I took out a paper and pencil. "When's the meeting?"

"It's a dinner thing. We'll be serving about six o'clock, and he'd start speaking about seven."

An evening gathering. Perfect. "I'll call him right now."

I contacted Harold. Of course, he was eager to speak. It was easy to make the arrangements. Dad was relieved when I told him everything was set.

"That's going to be a busy evening," Emily said.

I almost asked why, but I remembered. "That's right. Your bridal shower's that night, too. Starts about eight, doesn't it?" She confirmed the time.

"Gee, Dad, you mean you'd miss the bridal shower for a club meeting?" Everyone started laughing at Dad's mock look of horror.

We finished the logistics of the shower, the fittings, and the wedding rehearsal. I headed home. The adrenaline rush I'd missed so much started as I drove the car toward my apartment. I'd finally have a chance to look at the food bank computer!

After I got home, I sketched out some plans. I still had a key to the building, so my entry would be lawful. Harold would have to spend some time getting to the meeting and back. The meal, speech, and questions should take at least two hours. Looked like I'd have a clear three hours to play at the computer. I might be late to Emily's shower, but I'd do my best to be on time.

The next day, I hummed as I pulled out files for the day's work.

Tom passed by the desk. "You're awfully happy today. What's up?"

"Oh, you know, the wedding and everything." Couldn't very well tell him I was excited about hacking a computer.

"Nothing else?" I knew he was referring to Don.

"No, nothing else."

He seemed satisfied and went to his office.

The day of Dad's meeting, I took off work early. After donning my brown wig, I pulled the car out and headed toward the food bank. It felt good to be back trying to solve a case again, even if it was a small one. How I'd missed the cat-and-mouse game of good guy versus bad guy!

About 5:30 I parked across the street from the building and waited for Harold to come out. *Come on; come on. Get going.* Harold and Irene came out together, climbed in their vehicles and went their respective ways. I waited a few minutes more to make sure no one was coming back then scurried across the street to the back door.

I took the stairs to Harold's office two at a time, sat down, snapped on the desk light, and hit the computer switch. Soon the familiar screen came up, and I used Irene's login name and password to gain access to the software. There was nothing unusual or suspicious about the programs Irene worked with. After I finished clicking through her files, I realized I'd have to try to guess Harold's password information.

My shoulders sagged. This operation was going to take longer than I thought. I looked at my watch. Six o'clock. Good, I still had a few hours to play. I tried all kinds of different combinations of Harold's first and last names and came up with nothing for the login name. Then I had a hunch. I typed in the name Ernie. The computer liked that. Irene was right. Harold hadn't gotten over the young boy who was so tragically murdered.

It followed that the password would have something to do with Ernie. I searched the files for information on the kid and came up empty. Harold's desk was next. I found nothing on the first go-round, so decided to pull the drawers completely out. Tucked in one of the empty spaces was a worn manila folder. The file contained a standard form with information about an Ernest Townson. Something from the jacket fell to the floor. I picked up a photo of a young smiling boy, eager to look good for his school picture. It had to be Ernie.

I put the desk drawers back; then tried different bits of Ernie's data in the password field. I hit pay dirt with the numerals of his street address. Harold's hidden folders and programs flashed on the screen. My hand twitched on the computer mouse when I saw one particular folder. It was marked CRF.

As I clicked on it and saw the information, the whole setup was all too apparent. Harold had a secret bank account in another city that he was hiding money in for something called the Children's Relief Fund. He had undoubtedly skimmed money from the food bank to make his pet project possible.

I pulled out an empty floppy disk and began copying the file. As the information flew from one drive to the other, the enormity of the find began to dawn on me. My mind flashed back to the initials Cindy had written on that paper Clint had found in her apartment. It all fell into place. HC had to be Harold Carpenter. FBI was Food Bank of Indalia, and CRF certainly stood for Children's Relief Fund. Cindy must have suspected something was wrong with the books and had tried to figure out what was going on. I closed my eyes against a horrible thought. Was Cindy's death somehow connected to the hidden account?

As I stared at the computer screen, my ears strained at a sound.

Footsteps on the stairs.

CHAPTER 27

I yanked the disk out of the drive, turned off the desk light and computer then tiptoed to the closet. The only thing I could do now was hole up until Harold went to sleep, then sneak out.

There was a click, and the office light seeped under the closet door. I heard the desk chair creak, and the computer hummed to life again.

"Huh." The screen he was seeing surprised Harold. I hadn't had time to properly shut down the computer, and it was complaining to him. He rustled papers for a while, then I heard the desk chair roll back. Finally. He was going to bed.

He walked toward the door. I was almost home free. Almost. My pump beeped. Harold stopped moving. I could imagine him looking around the room to see what might have made the noise.

I pushed the backlight to see what the pump was trying to tell me. A No Delivery alarm was showing on the screen. What other alarms might sound while I was in this closet? I didn't need any other noises tipping Harold off that I was in the closet. I had to silence the pump somehow.

Putting the pump on Vibrate seemed like a good idea. I moved my arm—ready to push buttons. My elbow hit a small filing cabinet. The metallic thunk echoed in my ears like cymbals crashing together.

I heard the floorboards creak. Harold had heard the sound. He was walking toward the closet. I braced myself.

I blinked to accustom myself to the light after Harold yanked the door open. "Guess I shouldn't be surprised," he said as he pulled me out into the room. "Did you arrange that little speaking engagement so I'd be out of the way tonight?"

"Let's say the circumstances worked out well." I spoke calmly, not wanting him to think I was afraid of him.

"And are you the reason my computer showed it wasn't shut down properly?"

"Yes."

He shoved me into a chair. "Find anything interesting?"

"How could I? I couldn't break your login code."

"Really. Smart girl like you shouldn't have any trouble getting into an old junker computer." He put his face close to mine then pulled on my shoulders. "Stand up!"

He patted me down and found the floppy in my jacket. He waved the disk in front of my face. "What would I find on this, Claire?"

"Nothing. I told you I couldn't hack into the computer."

He smirked. "I wonder why I don't believe that. Maybe it's because you sneaked in here at night and hid in my closet."

Gripping my arm tightly, he moved us both back to the desk and turned on the computer again. After it warmed up, he slipped the disk into the floppy drive. My evidence lit up the screen.

His face contorted, he pulled the disk from the drive, laid it flat and dug at it with a letter opener. I backed up toward the door.

"Not so fast!" He came at me and put the opener blade against my windpipe. "You're not going anywhere!"

I had nothing to lose, so I asked the question. "Did Cindy find out about your little embezzlement scheme?"

He looked surprised, then his eyes narrowed. He guided me back to the desk and pushed me into his chair, all the time keeping the blade close to my neck.

"I might as well tell you what happened to Cindy. You'll soon be in no position to tell anyone."

"Was she on to you?"

"Yes. She started doing the books, and she wondered where some of the money was going. I wasn't as clever about hiding it in those days."

"Why did you start skimming in the first place? The children's center is a worthwhile project. Surely you eventually could have gotten the money together to build it."

"You've heard me arguing on the phone with our esteemed mayor. There was never enough money to budget for the center."

"What about the donations from the service clubs?"

"The clubs have been good to me, but Indalia isn't a big city. They couldn't raise enough money to get the job done as quickly as it needs to be finished."

"What's the hurry?"

"I already found one child dead with his brains and blood splattered all over the place. Ernie was everything to me. When I saw his body, I swore that, whatever it took, no other child was going to die that way." His face clouded, and he hung his head as he thought about Ernie. I tried easing the roller chair toward the door. The opener was back at my neck.

"Don't even think about it. You're not going anywhere until I'm ready."

"Okay, you're the boss." I put my hands up to calm him. "I'm going to make a giant leap in logic here and assume you killed Cindy. Why did you do it?"

He sat on the desk and stared down at me. "You probably won't believe this, but Cindy's death was an accident."

"Convince me."

"She was working late one night. I didn't know she was up here. I came back after dinner to do some work and heard a noise. I grabbed a two by four and came up to see what was going on."

His face paled. "She'd been looking over the books and had found the discrepancy. She wanted to know where the money was."

"What'd you tell her?"

"I told her about Ernie, about my plans for the center, but she didn't understand. She said she'd have to tell the city." He breathed faster. "She started toward the door, and my reflexes took over. In order to stop her, I hit her in the head with the board I had in my hand."

A picture of Cindy trying to do the right thing and being attacked for it played in my brain. It took a moment before I could speak. "The blow to her head didn't kill Cindy. Why did you think you had to throw her in the canal?"

"I panicked. I couldn't tell if she was dead or alive." Harold shifted position on the desk. "I figured if she was alive and regained consciousness, she'd tell the authorities. Everything I'd worked for would go down the drain." His eyes took on a pleading look. "You've got to understand. It was all for Ernie. Ernie was all that mattered. I couldn't let my work for his memory be in vain." His eyes filled with tears. "So I loaded her body in the trunk of my car, drove to the canal, weighted the body down, and threw her in." He put his face in his hands, reliving that awful night.

This was my chance. I leaped from the chair and ran for the door. He grabbed me from behind, and we struggled. I yelped as I felt the edge of the desk dig into my hip. I slammed him against the file cabinet.

He came at me again, and we rolled across the desk tangled in each other's bodies. The phone fell with a crash as we grappled with each other. We slid off the desk onto the floor.

Harold managed to wrap one arm around my body and clamped the other hand over my mouth and nose. I was surprised again at his power. His arms, strengthened by lifting boxes of food for the poor, were killing me.

I struggled to free myself, to breathe. I was desperate for air, clawing at his arms. My lungs screamed for oxygen. There had to be a way to break free, to get away from his vise-like grip. I kept struggling, but my movements grew weaker. Harold's grip loosened. There was a tremendous pain in my head, then blackness.

Little needles dug into my back. I rolled over to get away from the discomfort, and the prickles chafed my shoulder. After a few more minutes, I regained full consciousness.

As I propped myself to a sitting position, I could feel leaves and twigs beneath my hands. I could also feel one very sore spot on my head. My fingers explored the aching area. Harold must have hit me to make sure I was unconscious for a good while.

I staggered to my feet. Where was I? As my eyes became accustomed to the gloom, shapes became clear in the darkness. I could see trees all around me. Great. Harold had dumped me in the woods.

Something else wasn't right. I felt my waistband. My insulin pump was gone! Why? Was it detached in the fight? Had it fallen off in Harold's car? Then it dawned on me. Harold knew how my pump worked. Instead of dirtying his hands, he was going to let the lack of insulin kill me.

He'd left the tubing in place. I removed it from my abdomen. It was now not a source of life, but of infection.

How long had I been out? My watch was gone, no doubt torn off during the struggle. I was in deep trouble. No one knew where I was. I didn't even know where I was. My blood sugar was surely climbing. I had no emergency supplies. Could I find my way out of here? How much time did I have left? Was anyone looking for me?

Take it easy, Claire. I willed myself to take deep breaths and calm down. My sugar was climbing high enough already. I didn't need to make it worse by getting stressed out.

Determination kicked in. I swore if it was the last thing I did, I'd make it out and tell Don who killed Cindy.

The blood pounded in my ears from nerves. I had to wait for a few minutes for my pulse to slow so I could hear. Then I picked up a sound that was better than any symphony I'd ever listened to—the swoosh of cars driving on a highway.

I started toward the noise, but had to stop to pee. There are some advantages to being alone in the woods. I began walking again. Since I knew it would be easy to go in circles in the dark, I stopped periodically to check and make sure I was still headed in the right direction. As I continued my journey, I stumbled over fallen branches and scraped through densely packed trees—their bark seemed to reach out to attack me. I started feeling sick to my stomach.

There was something familiar about the way my body felt, then I realized I'd felt the same way when I was diagnosed with diabetes. My sugar had been running between 400 and 500 at the time. *Not a good sign, Claire.*

The car sounds were getting louder. *Hang on. You can make it.* I began feeling winded from the effort. I needed to take deep breaths to keep going. My head hurt. I wanted to vomit. My muscles ached, and my skin was raw from scrapes. I fell over a rock, and my ribs screamed at the impact when I hit the ground. I wanted to stop and just lay there.

Cindy's cheerleader photo popped into my mind. *Don't you dare give up! Betty needs to know who killed her daughter!*

I broke through the last bit of brush and stood at the edge of the highway. Cars sped by. Would one of them stop at night and pick up a disheveled woman who'd just walked out of the woods? I needed to find out in a hurry. I was running out of time.

An eighteen-wheeler's headlights lit up the road. As it got closer, I stepped out into the highway to wave it down. I felt so bad I didn't care if it ran over me.

The brakes screeched as the driver tried to stop before he hit me. I backed off a little, but not much. As soon as the truck stopped, I staggered to the passenger door, leaned on it for a second then opened it up.

"Lady, are you crazy?" the driver yelled.

All I saw was the blurry face of a man in a ball hat. "Diabetic…." I panted. "Take me … to hospital." I crawled up in the seat and passed out.

CHAPTER 28

"She's waking up."

I heard a familiar voice and opened my eyes. Someone was standing over me. When I could focus, I realized it was Mom.

"Claire, honey." She choked for a moment, then managed to speak again. "How do you feel?"

"Like I've been run over by a truck." My voice was raspy.

"You can thank a truck driver that you're alive." Dad took my hand. "He brought you to the emergency room."

I looked around, trying to orient myself. I was in a hospital room, an IV running full blast in my arm and a heart monitor attached to me. The last thing I remembered was collapsing in the truck. "What happened?"

"The driver brought you in." Dad drew a chair up to the bed. "You had no identification, so they didn't know who to call. Luckily Don was looking for you."

Don! "I need to see Don right away."

"Honey, I really think you need to rest now." Mom brushed the hair back from my forehead. "You can thank Don later."

"You don't understand." I grabbed at the bed's side rail and tried to sit up. "I know who killed Cindy Kagel. I need to tell Don now!"

"What!" Dad jumped out of his seat. "I'll get him. He's right outside."

When Don came in, he started asking how I was. I waved off his concern. "Don, does anyone from the press know I'm here?"

"No. Why do you ask?"

"Because you've got to pick up Harold Carpenter before he finds out I'm still alive." I went on to tell Don the whole story. "He's probably deleted all the computer records, but he hasn't had time yet to close out the hidden account." I told Don where the bank was located, and what name the account was under.

He sprinted for the door. "I want this collar myself. Thanks, Claire. I'll be back as soon as I can to tell you how it went."

I sank back into the pillow, exhausted. "Folks, is it okay with you if I get some sleep now?"

"Sure, honey." Dad patted my hand. "We'll be back later."

Even hooked up to monitors and IVs, I felt better than I had in a long time. Cindy was going to get her justice.

When Don came the next day, his smile was so big I thought his face was going to break.

"What's up?" I asked. "You look like you just ate the biggest canary that ever lived."

"What's up? Are you serious, Claire?" He pulled a chair over to the bedside. "I made the biggest collar of my career, thanks to you. That's what's up."

I rubbed my forehead. "You're going to have to forgive me. My mind's kind of hazy about what happened yesterday."

Don's eyes widened. "Don't you remember telling me that Harold Carpenter killed Cindy Kagel?"

I concentrated for a moment. Bits and pieces of what I'd told Don started coming back. "Ah, yes. Now it's coming back. How'd the arrest go?"

"It was sweet. I got some backup and went to the food bank. We nabbed Carpenter while he was still asleep." He leaned closer. "Just like you said, he hadn't had a chance to change accounts yet, so we have that evidence." Don's grin got even bigger.

"Of course, you'll need to testify if the case goes to trial."

"I'd be overjoyed to, but what do you mean 'if it goes to trial'?"

"The DA might plead it out. We'll see how it goes." He reached in his pocket. "I found something else on Carpenter's desk. I thought you might need it." He held up my pump. My day was complete.

Don pushed the chair back.. "By the way, there's someone outside who wants to see you." He opened the door and motioned for somebody to come in. It was Betty.

She walked toward me with arms outstretched. "How can I ever thank you?" We hugged.

"I'm glad for Cindy's sake that we got Carpenter." She stood up. I was wondering if I should ask the question at all, but the nosy side of my nature got the best of me. "What about Clint?"

"We, ah," Betty cleared her throat. "We may get back together. Clint's proved to me that he's making an effort at therapy. We'll see how it goes." She said her good-byes.

Don let her out, then came back to the bedside and took my hand.

"I understand you were looking for me. Why?" I asked.

"Seems you missed Emily's shower." He chuckled.

I put my hand to my mouth. "That's right. Somehow I forgot all about it." We both laughed. "So what happened?"

"From what I gather, your folks were mad at first. They thought you'd blown the whole thing off. Then they got worried when they couldn't reach you at your apartment. You obviously weren't answering your cell phone either." He squeezed my hand. "They called me when they couldn't locate you."

I squeezed back. "I'll bet that made your day. You probably wondered if the volcano had erupted again."

"The thought crossed my mind," he agreed. "I started doing the by-the-book police thing and went to all your regular hangouts. Dewey hadn't seen you, of course, and the center where your Mom and Dad said you worked was closed."

"So you couldn't pick up my trail, huh. What kind of detective are you?"

"Not so fast, Missy. I went down to the food bank and ran into Little Billy. He'd been trying to call you because he saw Carpenter loading something into his car. Carpenter was still out when I tried to get into the building to talk to him." Don's hand stroked my cheek. "That's when I put out the call to the rest of the force to be on the lookout for you. Later we got word that the emergency room had admitted an unidentified young woman in a diabetic coma." His eyes moistened as he looked into mine. "On the way over, I prayed it was you."

We didn't speak for a while. We sat, looking at each other, really seeing each other—joyful at being together.

Don finally broke the silence. "Claire, when we couldn't find you, it scared me to death. I realized then that I need to be with you." He bent down and kissed my forehead. "Can we start over?"

Tears flowed down my cheeks. My throat tightened, and my voice was hoarse, but I managed to rasp out a yes as I caressed his cheeks and pulled his lips to mine.

My recovery was uneventful. The folks brought newspapers in while I was laid up. Of course, there were many articles about Harold Carpenter and Cindy's murder. The reporters also wrote about Carpenter's dream of a children's center in West Indalia.

The publicity and the obvious need for such a facility prompted the city council to okay using the funds Harold had squirreled away for that purpose. Harold would see his dream fulfilled even though it looked like he'd spend the rest of his life behind bars.

Newspaper coverage was also helping me. I was mentioned prominently as the person who cracked the case. I decided to open up my office again.

One day as I was unpacking boxes with Respighi playing on the CD, Don stopped by. "Hi, handsome." I sidled up to him. "Want to help?"

"No thanks." He shied away from the cartons of paperwork. "It's my day off. I came down to take you for a drive."

"Oh yeah. Where are we going?"

"You'll see." He opened the office door. "Come on. I want to show you something."

We drove to West Indalia. "I need to see this part of town? What's up, Don?"

"Be patient." He parked the car, and we got out.

We walked to an empty lot where construction workers were busy. We stood, hand in hand, watching them. Then Don pointed to a sign. I read it and got a lump in my throat. There in black glossy letters shining out from a white background, the sign proclaimed—Future Home of the Cynthia Kagel Children's Center.

THE END

Printed in the United States
47717LVS00001B/145-165